A DARLING AVIATOR

DARLING MEN
BOOK TWO

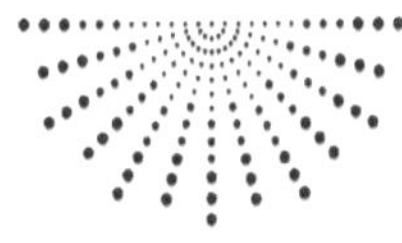

LARK HOLIDAY

GLASS ELEPHANT PRESS

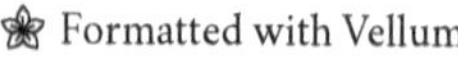 Formatted with Vellum

To Danelle, for teaching me what it means to be a true hero. Thank you for saving me so many times that I lost count. Thank you for leading by example when so many others just talk. Thank you for reminding me that there is a reason why we're here. That even if we don't know the reason, it still exists.

The only problem is that you set the standard too high.

CHAPTER ONE

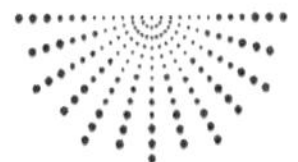

MAC

"I am serious, Mac. Your best behavior."

Maverick Carter scowled at his younger sister. As if he didn't know how to act at thirty-five years old. "What exactly is wrong with my behavior?"

Sarah raised an eyebrow. "Ever hear you catch more flies with honey?"

Mac snorted. "That's assuming I want to catch flies at all. You know I prefer my space."

"Oh, really?" Sarah pointed to where Bart, her small white terrier mix, sat at Mac's feet.

"A dog is different."

"Different from what? A girlfriend?"

"Jesus Christ." His shoulders hunched together. Ever since Sarah had gotten into a relationship, she hadn't stopped hinting at Mac to do the same. Just because it had happened for her, she acted like it was possible for everyone else. But life didn't work that way. "Why can't I just work in peace?"

"You can always file a complaint with the HR department." Sarah tapped her chin. "Oh, wait, that's me."

Mac glanced up at the cloudless blue sky, praying for the patience to get through one day without arguing with his sister. It was an occupational hazard of helping out at their family's lodge. "Look, just let me worry about myself, okay? Anyway, if my behavior was so awful, would I be here fixing the van right now?"

Sarah's smile disappeared. "Is it even fixable?"

Mac tucked his head back under the hood. At over six feet tall, he didn't exactly fit comfortably. "I hope so."

"Hope?" Her voice was strained. "I need a little more than hope right now."

He shot Sarah a sideways glance. With her arms resting on her hips like that and her pregnant belly in the middle, she looked like a teapot. Mac kept the observation to himself, figuring it wouldn't improve her mood much. "What's so special about this guest?"

Sarah's gaze flicked to the side. "What do you mean?"

With a sigh, Mac moved back out from under the hood and straightened to look her in the eye. It was only last year that Sarah had moved back to the small Alaskan island where they had both grown up. But even after years apart, Mac could still read his sister like a book. Something was going on. "You aren't trying to set me up with her, are you?"

Sarah burst out laughing, clutching her chest. "Set you up with Elle Blessing? No way. I want her to have a good time, not scare her away. And unlike you, she's not determined to be single forever. She's coming here with her fiancé."

Mac narrowed his eyes. He wasn't a fan of Sarah meddling with his dating life, but did she have to laugh at him? He wasn't that awful. Right? "Then what's the big deal?"

Sarah shifted to her other foot. "She's famous."

"She an actress or something?"

"An influencer," she told him. "Her platform is mostly focused on food, and she creates a lot of her own recipes."

Mac barked a laugh. "That's not a real job."

Sarah glared at him. "Yes, it is. She has millions of followers."

He shrugged. "You know I don't care about that crap."

"Well, you should." Sarah spread her arms wide, gesturing to the lodge. "One post from Elle and this place could be booked out for the next decade. But that's only going to happen if she has a good time." Sarah gave him a pointed look. "Which includes you being nice."

He pressed his lips together. Now Sarah wanted to change everything about their family business too? He liked it better when she was just focused on his dating life. "We're doing just fine without her."

Sarah rested her hands on her rounded tummy. "I want more than fine."

Mac clenched his jaw. Goddammit. Why did she have to do that? "Whatever. I'll do it. But you can't play the pregnancy card again."

Sarah beamed. She knew she had him. Once Mac made a promise, he never broke it. "And you'll wear the hat?"

He drew the line at the hat. "Absolutely not. This is a lodge in Alaska. If people want uniforms, they can go to a theme park."

The front door of the lodge swung open, and Sarah's husband, Will, stepped outside. He raised his arm in greeting as he walked over to them. "How's it going out here?"

With a grunt, Mac turned back to the van.

"What were you just saying about your best behavior?" Sarah hissed.

Mac sucked in a deep breath before straightening and offering Will a wave.

The truth was that Sarah's husband wasn't that bad. At

first, Mac had figured all of Will's good intentions about sticking around in Alaska would evaporate the minute the first snow fell. He was the definition of a city boy.

But Will had stayed strong, and his first winter was behind him already. They were knee-deep in spring now, and summer was practically blowing them all a kiss. This was the time of year when people fell in love with Alaska.

Mac nodded in Will's direction. "It's going. You?"

Will smiled as he slid an arm around Sarah's waist, or tried to. It wasn't exactly an easy maneuver now that she was almost at her due date. "Couldn't be better."

A twinge of jealousy flared in Mac's heart. It wasn't that he wasn't happy for Sarah and Will. He was. His sister deserved a good life.

Not to mention that since Sarah and Will had taken over running the Salmonberry Lodge, life had gotten better for the whole family. Sarah and Mac's parents had been able to take their first vacation in decades and were in Italy for the summer. Meanwhile, Mac had been able to focus almost solely on his flight business.

Besides picking up passengers for the lodge, he flew people out to nearby islands for fishing trips and to the mainland, connecting flights to the lower forty-eight. Sometimes, he flew cargo. He liked flying stuff. It didn't talk.

But the truth was that from time to time, Mac did crave female company. He wasn't celibate by any measure of the imagination, but a relationship was a lot different than a fling.

Unfortunately, wanting something didn't make it magically happen. There were few women on the island to begin with, and most were either already married or his mom's age. Those Mac had grown up with had left town at their first chance.

Besides, dating a local came with its own set of problems.

Like what if things went south? The idea of running into his theoretical ex every day wasn't exactly tempting.

Sarah had gotten lucky with Will. That almost never happened. As a general rule, a person either came to Darling with someone or stayed single. Mac had been firmly in the second category all his life.

"How's the van looking?" Will asked.

Mac sighed. "I'm pretty sure it needs a new alternator. I'll pick one up next time I'm in Juneau."

Sarah's face fell. "But Elle is getting here tomorrow!"

Mac ran the back of his hand across his forehead, wiping away the sweat. It was rare that it got above sixty degrees on the island, and it felt hot as hell. Today was the kind of day that made cruise ship passengers uproot the family and move to Alaska when they got home.

He pitied them. Those poor fools had no idea that it rained easily a hundred inches a year, and they just happened to catch one of the good days. "So refund her and call it a day. Or did you forget you're having a baby in two weeks?"

"We're ready for that when the time comes." Sarah stuck her chin out. "And we didn't take any other reservations this season."

Mac gritted his teeth. "Yeah, so you can take care of yourself and the baby. Not so we can wait hand and foot on some spoiled brat."

Sarah stepped closer to Mac, resuming the teapot pose with a hand on each hip. Will stayed put, apparently knowing better than to get between the two Carter siblings by now. While they shared the same auburn hair and green eyes, the main thing Mac and Sarah had in common was how stubborn they both could be. "This is a once-in-a-lifetime opportunity, and I don't intend to pass on it." She tipped her head up, looking him in the eye. "Don't you ever want more, Mac?"

On the outside, he didn't flinch. But inside, his stomach twisted. Of course he wanted more. Except Mac knew better than to ask for it. He'd rather not ask than be disappointed. "Have it your way. I'll drive them to the lodge in my truck."

Mac slammed the hood of the van shut and scooped up his toolbox. After giving Bart a quick pat on the head, Mac walked to his truck. He was done with this conversation.

"Are you kidding me?" Sarah called after him. "You can't drive them in your truck! The goal is to make a good impression. Which is going to be impossible in that rusty piece of shit!"

Mac turned, giving her a sarcastic smile. "Then I'll wear the stupid-ass hat. That ought to distract them."

He set the toolbox in the truck bed and climbed into the driver's seat. If Elle Whoever didn't like it, she could go back to where she came from. Mac didn't give a rat's ass if she enjoyed Alaska or not.

Pressing down on the gas pedal, Mac pulled out onto the road and headed back in the direction of town. He glanced up at the rearview mirror, glimpsing the Salmonberry Lodge growing smaller behind him.

Mac shifted in his seat. Dammit. Now he felt guilty. He shouldn't give Sarah crap like that, not when she was about to pop. But all that talk about things changing pissed him off.

Was it so wrong that he knew what he wanted? That was more than most people could say.

He wanted this life right here. There wasn't anything else he was suited for. The confidence and skill to fly, the resilience to make it through long winter nights, and, most demanding of all, the patience of putting up with a small town that was always in his business.

Mac tightened his grip on the steering wheel as the truck bumped along the gravel road. Of all the reasons he stayed single, that was the big one.

He knew what he wanted, and he knew that no one else wanted the same thing.

Mac had seen what his parents had given up to live in Darling. What it had cost them. Once they left the East Coast for the last frontier, their families had never spoken to them again. Even if Mac ever had the guts to ask someone to make the same choice, he knew better than to believe for a second that someone would pick him.

As Mac pulled into town, the thick forest trees fell back from the road. Worn wooden buildings in faded colors sat on either side of Main Street. The only street in town, really. A dirty SUV drove past him, followed by a truck that had been new twenty years ago.

The whole town, and all the people in it, had seen better days.

Mac turned the corner to the workshop that doubled as his home. He could only imagine that for a person not suited to this life, it would be torture. The same routine, day in and day out. The same small world.

He sighed. For all of Sarah's talk about change, there was one thing that would always stay the same.

He would be single forever.

CHAPTER TWO

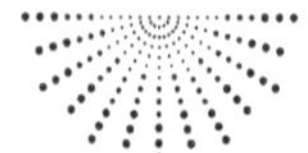

ELLE

There was only one part of this trip that Elle Blessing was looking forward to.

Going home.

Once she was back in Los Angeles, Elle was never getting on a plane again. She was definitely never coming back to Alaska. She hated the cold. And the next time Travis insisted on an outdoor adventure, Elle would find a way to convince him to do it without her.

She glanced at her fiancé, sleeping soundly in the seat next to her.

Guilt prodded at her stomach. But this trip wasn't about what she wanted. It was about doing something for Travis after he had done so much for her.

Elle pried one hand off the armrest and glanced at her smartwatch. Only thirty more minutes until they landed in Ketchikan. Thirty more minutes, followed by the longest five days and four nights of her life.

She swallowed. When Travis had first told Elle about the

Salmonberry Lodge, she had thought it was a great idea—for his bachelor party. After all, his friend Chris was the one who had stayed at the lodge last summer and raved about it. Why not go with him?

But Travis had insisted he wanted to take the trip with Elle and have some quality time together. How could she say no?

A ding sounded in the cabin as the seat belt sign came on, followed by a series of clicks as the passengers prepared to land.

Elle had never taken her seat belt off in the first place. How the heck was everyone else so calm about barreling through the air in a metal tube? Didn't they realize that it only took one small thing to go wrong, and they would all be toast?

She took a deep breath. Once they landed, Elle would be able to focus on enjoying the trip with Travis. Or at least trying to for his sake.

All she needed was a hot shower, and Elle would feel like a new person. She hadn't stopped sweating since they had gotten on the plane.

When they had first started dating, Elle had told Travis she was a nervous flier. Except back then, she had been so worried about what he would think of her that she may have toned down her fear of flying. A lot.

Luckily, work had kept her too busy to travel much anyway. Elle hadn't taken a day off since she first started her social media accounts eight years ago.

Her work demanded her constant attention. As her manager reminded Elle all the time, someone would replace her in a second. There was always someone younger, prettier, skinnier, blonder. All it would take was letting her guard down for one second, and people would forget the name Elle Blessing altogether.

She closed her eyes, but that only made her stomach churn. She snapped her eyes open, checking the time again.

Elle groaned. How the heck had it only been three minutes?

With a shaky breath, she stretched over Travis's shoulder to peek out the window. She'd feel better if she could see land. Land meant this was almost over.

Elle frowned. All she could see was a bunch of trees and water so dark blue that it was almost black. What was so great about this place?

Too bad she couldn't hire whatever marketing team Alaska had because she seemed to be the only person in the world who didn't get the appeal.

She sat back in her seat.

Focus on what you can control.

Her mind instantly went back to work. Elle had promised Travis that she wouldn't work the entire time they were in Alaska. But he understood that she couldn't disappear from social media completely either.

Especially not while she was in discussions with a popular streaming service about a possible miniseries. If the deal went through, the show could take Elle from being known for her recipes to a lifestyle brand complete with merchandise.

After all, wasn't that the point? To always reach the next level, no matter what? If she didn't keep growing, everything she had built would shrivel up and disappear. It didn't matter how hard she worked. How exhausted she was. She could never stop being Elle Blessing.

She touched her forehead, where a few fine lines had already started to show. Her manager had tried to push her towards getting her face touched up more than once. Elle knew where the worry lines had come from. Their namesake.

That's why she needed Travis. She handled the details and the worries. In return, he was a calming presence, a touchstone in the chaos that came with being an influencer.

Elle spent her life wound up so tight that Chihuahuas would howl as she walked by. Travis was the polar opposite. She had never seen him so much as wrinkle an eyebrow in concern.

Not to mention that she wouldn't know how to do all this without Travis, even if she wanted to. He had been there since the beginning. In a way, he had been the beginning.

The plane dropped suddenly before stabilizing, and a collective gasp came from the cabin.

Elle's hand shot out, gripping Travis's knee.

I'm going to be so pissed if I die in Alaska. I never even wanted to come here in the first place.

The captain's voice crackled over the intercom, apologizing for the turbulence.

Travis blinked his eyes open, glancing first at her hand and then up at Elle. "What's wrong?"

Her heart pounded, her breath shallow. "Just got startled. Turbulence."

"It's nothing to be worried about." Travis covered her hand with his, giving it a squeeze.

Her underarms prickled with sweat. "Sorry to bother you."

"You never bother me." Travis rubbed his thumb over the platinum ring on her finger. "We're a team, remember?"

Elle nodded as her throat grew tight, still not used to the heavy diamond.

Her followers had sure liked the news, though, and her numbers had shot through the roof since she'd announced that Travis had been upgraded from boyfriend to fiancé. "You're right."

Travis brushed a kiss against her cheek. "The trip will be more fun once we're at the lodge."

She smiled at him. He had done it again. Taken away her worries and left her with that stable, calm feeling.

No one knew what it was really like between the two of them. Not her manager. Not her followers. Not even his parents.

But no one needed to know. What she and Travis had was so much better than love. They understood each other.

She took her hand back, latching onto the armrest again. "Just one more connection, and we'll be there."

He grinned, and his face stayed smooth. Of course it did. Not only was he three years younger than her at twenty-five, Travis had never had anything to worry about. "Chris says this place is dope. It's like you have the whole island to yourself. There's nothing there. It's totally chill."

Elle forced a small smile. It sounded god-awful. But Travis wanted this, and she wanted him to be happy. "I can't wait."

As the plane descended and the pressure grew in her ears, the fine details of trees and rocks and a few buildings came into view.

Elle bit the inside of her cheek. It didn't look much better close-up than it had from far away.

Rain splattered against the window, and Travis turned to her. "Did you pack my rain jacket?"

Elle nodded. Travis hadn't even owned a rain jacket, but she had bought him one for this trip after researching what they would need. "Yep. It's packed."

"You're the best." Travis reached out to pat her thigh as they circled the airport. "This is going to be great. The trip of a lifetime."

"I'm sure you're right." She sat back in her seat. "Let's just hope the next flight is better. I hate turbulence."

The airplanes had gotten progressively smaller, more cramped, and less luxurious since they had left LAX this morning. Once they arrived in Ketchikan, Elle half expected the original plane invented by the Wright Brothers to be waiting for the last leg of their trip.

"It will be," Travis said. "I promise."

Elle gave him a small smile. She didn't believe in promises. Most of the time, it felt like the only person she could count on was herself. But she could believe her fiancé if no one else. Elle knew she could rely on Travis to be there at the end of the day, no matter what.

She forced slow, deep breaths as the plane grew closer to the runway.

This was going to be fine. She was overthinking things. Elle could survive a few days in Alaska. Then they would be back in LA, she'd close the deal on the miniseries, and she and Travis would get married after a respectable three years of dating.

Elle was going to win the game of life. How she felt had nothing to do with it.

CHAPTER THREE

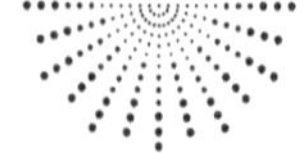

MAC

Mac stood outside his plane, waiting for the next flight from Seattle to arrive.

Yesterday's sunshine was long gone, replaced with the constant steady mist that blanketed southeast Alaska more often than not. Around here, rain boots were the footwear of choice, and almost everyone had a car door turn rusty on them at one point or another.

He liked this time of year. The island had finally shaken off winter, but cruise ship traffic hadn't jammed up every-thing yet.

Mac wasn't a fool, and he knew that the entire state depended on tourism. But that didn't mean he had to like it.

Especially this influencer person.

Mac cracked his neck. He intended to keep his promise to Sarah and be on his best behavior. But seeing the way this lady was stressing out his pregnant sister made him not like her already. And didn't Sarah know by now that counting on other people was setting herself up for disappointment?

A dull, droning noise turned into a roar as a plane appeared. It descended until the wheels tapped on the runway with a bounce, slowing to a stop.

With a sigh, Mac pulled the crumpled Salmonberry Lodge baseball cap from his coat pocket. He didn't have to wear it. He hadn't agreed to it, and Sarah would never know the difference. But after giving her a hard time yesterday, he felt the need to atone.

Mac cringed as he tugged it on. Stupid-ass hat. What was the point? He had never had a problem spotting guests before.

The tourists always dressed like an ad for an outdoor clothing company with their pristine gear. They wore bright colors and puffy parkas with faux-fur hoods. No one around here had that kind of money, and even if they did, there was no place to buy stuff like that anyway.

The ground crew wheeled up the stairs, and Mac walked over to meet up with the guests for the lodge.

As people poured out of the plane, Mac glanced at his watch. He was more than ready to get going. He had been early, like always, and the flight had been a few minutes late. If Mac was going to wait around and kill time, he preferred to do it with a cold beer in his hand.

Mac looked up just as a woman stepped off the plane.

He sucked in his breath.

Her golden hair managed to shine despite the cloudy day, and even from here, he could see she had blue eyes. Her form-fitting fleece and jeans hinted at a figure that looked like it had been conceived in a painting, something too perfect to be human.

Mac shifted his stance. Maybe he needed a vacation. It wasn't a good sign that he was getting worked up over a random stranger.

As the woman stepped forward, a man appeared behind

her. She turned to look at him with a smile, touching his arm. The diamond on her finger winked in the bright glare of the overcast day, taunting Mac.

He straightened. Of course a woman like her was taken. So much for that little fantasy. Mac wasn't one for relationships anyway, and he definitely drew the line at getting involved in other people's.

He kept his gaze glued on the plane, or tried to, as the couple walked in front of him.

He shivered. God. She smelled good too. Like flowers. *Focus.*

She stepped past him, then stopped and turned around.

Mac blinked. She was walking up to him, the man in tow.

The woman looked equally unsure, glancing around before her gaze landed back on him.

Shit.

Mac looked back at the other passengers. Surely it couldn't be them? There was no way this was his pickup.

"Maverick Carter?" Her voice tinkled like a wind chime. She pointed at his hat. "From the Salmonberry Lodge?"

Mac nodded. The few words he usually had to offer were not available. He hadn't expected to pick up an angel.

"I'm Elle." She turned and smiled at the man, resting a hand on his arm. "This is my fiancé, Travis. We're here for our flight to the lodge."

Mac swallowed. This wasn't happening. He shook hands with Travis. "Call me Mac. Nice to meet you."

Then he turned to Elle. Her hand was about a third of the size of his, but her grip more than made up for it.

Mac's stomach felt warm, and he kept the handshake shorter than he would've liked.

It didn't matter how gorgeous she was. She was engaged, and Mac had morals. In a week, these people would be out of his life and never look back.

He cracked a smile, remembering his promise to Sarah. "Ready for the best week of your life?"

* * *

About fifteen minutes after meeting Elle, Mac decided she didn't come from heaven. Hell was a more likely origin.

It was a much-needed reminder of why he didn't involve himself with women, particularly beautiful women. They were too much damn work.

Mac's plane was the first problem.

"Are you sure we can fit?" Elle wrinkled her perfect pixie nose.

Travis gave her a lazy smile. "It'll be fine, babe. I promise."

Mac raised an eyebrow. The man had to be stoned because he didn't seem to be picking up on Elle's anxiety at all.

But it wasn't Mac's first time around a nervous flier. "Look, if I can fit, you can fit."

Surely she could see the logic. Elle was over a foot shorter than him and definitely much less wide. Her fiancé wasn't much bigger than her, truth be told.

"I'm just not sure." She played with the ring on her finger.

Mac sighed. "I'll make it work, okay? It's never been a problem before."

Elle scrunched her brows together. "And you've done this a lot?"

Mac clenched his jaw. Losing his cool wouldn't make Elle any more eager to get on the plane. In his experience, the best approach with nervous fliers was to keep the ball rolling and get the flight over with. Dragging things out always made them worse. "All my life. Now, let's go get your luggage."

Elle hesitated. "We might need a cart."

"A cart?" Mac scoffed. Did she think he was some kind of weakling? He wasn't one of those pretty boys from the lower forty-eight who couldn't carry his own bags. "If you carried it to the airport, I can carry it to my plane. Be right back."

He walked over to where they had offloaded all the luggage onto a trailer. Mac looked over the pile and turned to the two guys loading up the suitcases. "I need the bags for Elle Blessing and Travis Briggs."

One of the men gestured to a cart so overloaded that it looked like it would topple over if a raven so much as landed on it. "That's it."

Mac walked over to the tower of bags. "In this pile?"

"No." The man shook his head. "That's it. The whole thing."

"No way in hell." Mac checked one tag and then another. They all had Elle's name. "Damn."

He unzipped his coat, his body as hot as his temper. Mac stomped back over to where Elle sat.

She scrambled to her feet when she saw him. "Is everything okay?"

Mac worked his jaw. "Is there a reason you brought your entire house?"

Elle frowned. "My house? That's my equipment."

"Equipment? For what? Oh, I know." Mac gave an exaggerated nod. "To build a new house."

"No." Her voice was strained. "For work."

Mac gritted his teeth, his promise increasingly difficult to keep. But he'd be damned if he broke his word. "You know this is supposed to be a vacation, right? No one expects you to earn your keep while you're here. You can just relax."

Travis rested an arm across Elle's shoulders. "That's my girl. She never stops working."

"It's true. I never take a day off." She smiled at Travis,

suddenly sweet as honey. "Although I did promise I would try to not work as much during our special trip."

Mac clenched his fists. "Okay, fine. Then you have a decision to make. What gets an extended stay at the airport? Your personal bags or your work stuff? I'm only making one flight today."

If he spent any more time than necessary around this woman, he was going to lose his cool. Everything about her pushed his buttons.

Her eyes grew wide. "You can't be serious. So, what, I choose my work bags, and we can't shower or anything?"

With a shiver, Mac mentally sped past the idea of her in the shower. Where presumably she'd have no clothes on. "Here's the deal. I don't have enough light to fly back today, not with the time it would take to refuel. I'll bring the rest of your stuff to the lodge tomorrow." He folded his arms. "So what do you want?"

Elle bit her lip, glancing at Travis. He shrugged. "I understand you need your work stuff. We can make it a day without our bags. We'll still have a great time."

She shook her head. "No, we're here to have fun." Elle looked back at Mac. "My work stuff can wait until tomorrow."

He jerked his thumb in the direction of the luggage cart. "Want to come show me which bags you need today?"

Now that she had made a decision, he didn't want to give her a chance to change her mind. Mac couldn't stand when people didn't know what they wanted. It wasn't that hard to make a choice.

Elle nodded and left Travis's side to follow behind Mac. He glanced back. Travis had trailed behind them a bit, stopping halfway between the luggage and the plane. Interesting. Not only was Elle a workaholic, but she was also a ballbuster.

She pointed out the suitcases with their personal items, and Mac told the guys he'd be back for everything else tomorrow.

Mac picked up both bags, even though Elle insisted she could carry her own. So far, she wasn't doing a very good job of being on vacation.

Her forehead wrinkled, and Mac's shoulders pinched together. Jesus Christ, what now? "Something wrong?"

Elle glanced back at the luggage cart. "Are you sure my stuff will be safe?"

He sighed. "Perfectly safe. They have a storage room. And even if something happens, you can't just take a week off?"

She looked up at him, her blue eyes so full of worry that Mac almost felt bad for her. "I don't know what I would do."

He held her gaze. "I'll get that stuff to you tomorrow. Okay? I promise."

Elle nodded, but her forehead stayed crisscrossed with lines.

That was fine. She didn't know the power of a Maverick Carter promise yet.

They made their way back to where Travis waited, and Mac led the two of them over to his plane.

He glanced back to make sure they were still following him. The couple walked with about a foot of space between the two of them and didn't hold hands.

Weird. Mac had never been engaged, but didn't people usually act cozier than that? His sister and Will were so lovey-dovey with each other that it made Mac want to barf. Sometimes the two of them even seemed to have a conversation without speaking a word at all. That really chapped his ass.

Mac shrugged it off. Whatever. Travis and Elle's relationship was none of his business. It didn't matter that Elle was gorgeous. She was engaged. Mac would never cross that line.

Even if she was available, Elle was no different than any other woman from the lower forty-eight. Not a single one of them would want to spend her life with a quiet man in rural Alaska.

It was too much to ask of someone. So Mac never asked at all.

CHAPTER FOUR

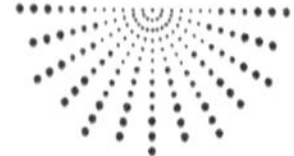

So much for this flight being better.

The little plane was cramped and loud, with a constant droning noise that Elle could hear even through the earmuffs that doubled as a headset.

Her chest grew tight as the cabin seemed to close in around her. How much longer until they got there?

Elle glanced back at Travis. She had tried to give him the front seat so he had a better view, but Mac had grumbled something about weight distribution and stuck her in front.

On the bright side, Travis seemed thrilled regardless. After his nap on the flight from Seattle, he was as perky as a puppy.

He kept tapping her on the shoulder and pointing at something outside the window. Elle smiled and nodded every time, even though she never knew what she was supposed to be looking at. It was all the same to her. But if he was happy, Elle could be happy.

The plane shook, and Elle gripped the sides of her seat

with both hands. Her heart pounded as her palms turned sweaty.

She stared at Mac, waiting for some kind of reassurance. Even the faceless pilot on the flight from Seattle had apologized.

After a few moments, Mac glanced her way. "What?"

Elle gaped at him. "What was that?"

Annoyance flashed in his eyes. "That? You don't mean the turbulence, do you? You've been on about a million flights today. Shouldn't be anything new by now."

She pressed her lips together and faced forward, her stomach churning. Elle had dreaded this trip since she had booked it. Her first impressions of Alaska weren't helping.

In her head, she again counted down the days until they would be back in their condo in Los Angeles. She already missed the floor-to-ceiling windows and the view of the sprawling skyline. She missed the sunshine and the warmth.

Elle missed the world she knew.

Mac cleared his throat, his voice crackling in the headset. "I'm doing my best to avoid it. Okay?"

She nodded. That was probably as close as she was going to get to an apology. "Thanks."

Elle wanted to say more. She wanted to say how terrified she was. How she didn't even want to be here. But Travis could hear every word she spoke in his headset too, and she didn't want him to think she wasn't having a good time.

Mac flashed her a quick smile, or that's what she assumed it was supposed to be. It looked more like he had a toothache. "I haven't crashed yet."

She shifted in her seat. That didn't necessarily make her feel better. But if he was going to extend her an olive branch, she could at least take it. "I'm sure if you keep trying, one of these days, you just might succeed."

Mac let out a huff that may have been a laugh, and Elle smiled. Travis never laughed at her jokes.

Elle gulped. That must be the fear talking. There was no way in hell she had just compared Mac to Travis. There was no comparison. Travis was everything Mac was not.

Her gaze dropped to the ring on her finger. Travis was one of the best things that ever happened to her. It wasn't just that he was rich and good-looking. It wasn't the fact that dating LA royalty had skyrocketed her career overnight after five years of struggling.

It was that they understood each other. Even after the chemistry had faded, Travis stayed by her side. What they had was something that worked. Something she could depend on.

And love? That she could live without. Her parents had married for love and spent the rest of their lives struggling. Elle might not have many good memories from growing up, but she had at least learned a valuable lesson. Love didn't last. Love cost too much.

A few minutes later, they circled an island where a few ramshackle old buildings were clustered together.

Elle craned her neck to get a better view. This could not possibly be Darling. Darling sounded quaint and homey. This place looked abandoned.

Her stomach sank. Poor Travis. He had been so excited for this trip. She turned, ready to comfort him.

But Travis didn't need any comforting. He grinned, practically bouncing in his seat. "We're almost there."

Elle gave him a tight smile and trained her gaze out of the window again. That was even worse, somehow. Travis didn't realize how awful this actually was. But this was his vacation, and as long as he was enjoying himself, she was determined to do the same.

Mac didn't bother announcing their landing. Customer

service clearly wasn't his specialty. But why would it be? He probably had the monopoly on flights on this crappy little island. There couldn't be much competition. There didn't appear to be much of anything.

As they flew closer to the water, Elle squeezed her eyes shut. Hopefully, Mac wasn't lying when he said he knew what he was doing. If not, she'd find out in about five seconds.

Her eyes snapped open as the plane touched down, gliding to a stop. Elle's stomach turned over, unused to the feeling between a plane and a boat.

Meanwhile, Travis giggled like a little kid, loving every moment.

Her body sagged with relief. They had landed. She was done with planes for today. And Travis was happy. As far as this trip went, she couldn't ask for more than that.

The plane made a turn and headed back to shore. It came to a stop, bumping against the dock.

Mac jumped out and secured the plane. He opened her door and spread his arms wide. "Welcome to Darling."

Based on his dry tone, she doubted just how welcome they really were.

Elle reached one leg out, tentatively feeling for the dock with her foot. All she wanted was to be on solid ground. Just when she thought she'd found it, the dock bobbed, and she tripped forward out of the plane.

She let out a squeal as she jerked to a stop in midair.

With the reflexes of a cat, Mac caught her, one arm wrapped almost completely around her waist and one holding her hand. She was halfway between a fall and a waltz.

Mac's jade eyes searched hers. "You okay?"

Elle nodded, her heart pounding, and Mac helped her to her feet.

He let go to offer a hand to Travis, and a chill seeped through her.

Shivering, Elle wrapped her arms around herself and gazed down at the blue-black water lapping against the dock.

The honest truth was that she was far from okay. And Mac was the first person to ask her that in a long time.

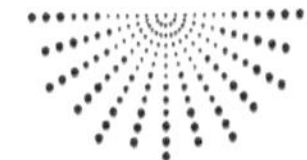

CHAPTER FIVE

MAC

His sister had lost her damned mind.

Mac held the suitcases, frozen on the spot. What the hell had Sarah done to the lodge?

The knotty pine handrail was covered in bright pink crepe paper. A sparkly welcome banner hung from the ceiling. And several bunches of pink balloons dotted the room, tied down to the rustic wood furniture. It looked god-awful.

Mac didn't know whether to laugh or be terrified. This must be some misdirected form of nesting.

Elle had barely stepped foot inside when Sarah wrapped her in an awkward hug, reaching around her giant belly. "Welcome to the Salmonberry Lodge!"

Mac just stared. They were handing out hugs now? He had agreed to be on his best behavior, but he drew the line at physical affection.

He shifted his feet, irked at how good it had felt to hold Elle. He'd have to wash the memory away with a drink later.

She was an engaged woman, and Mac wouldn't touch that with a ten-foot pole.

As they broke apart, Sarah gasped and grabbed Elle's hand. "Oh my God. Your ring is even more gorgeous in real life."

Elle's forehead wrinkled. "Excuse me?"

Mac watched the scene unfold like a car crash he couldn't tear his gaze away from. After all the crap Sarah had given him about being on his best behavior, it turned out she was the one dropping the ball.

Sarah's face turned red, and she glanced at Mac before looking back at Elle. "I, uh, don't mean to sound creepy. I follow you on social media."

"It's always great to meet a follower." Elle gave her a reassuring smile. "I just hadn't expected anyone up here to know who I am."

Sarah's face relaxed into a grin. "Are you kidding? The most beloved couple on the internet? Of course I know who you are! We are so excited to have you here."

"Thank you so much. We've been looking forward to this." Elle turned to her fiancé. "Right, honey?"

Travis nodded. "Totally. This place is awesome."

"We have done a lot of work recently." Sarah beamed. "I had been in LA myself until last year, but my husband and I live here now to help my parents."

"They must be so happy." Elle pointed to Sarah's tummy. "Especially with a grandchild on the way."

Sarah rubbed her belly. "Their first."

Elle smiled. "Congratulations."

"I should tell you the same thing. I can't wait to hear all about the wedding." Sarah got a dreamy look in her eye. "I love weddings."

Mac shifted on his feet. This conversation was putting

him to sleep. He didn't get why women went gaga for weddings. The only good part was the open bar.

Travis took Elle's hand. "You might be the first to know the details. We haven't had time to discuss it. Maybe we can do that here."

Elle's smile turned brittle. She didn't look thrilled about that plan. "Great idea."

Sarah clapped her hands together. "How about a glass of champagne to celebrate?"

Mac lifted an eyebrow. Hugs *and* champagne? What the hell was this? Therapy?

Elle rested a hand on her fiancé's arm. "I'm not much of a drinker, but maybe Travis would like some."

Sarah's brows squished together. "Is there anything else you would like? Iced tea? Orange juice? Coffee? Anything at all."

Elle's gracious smile returned. "You know what? Maybe I will have a splash of champagne."

Sarah's face relaxed again. Interesting. So Elle wasn't totally spoiled or at least had enough common sense not to stress out a pregnant lady. That was more than Mac would've given her credit for. "Fantastic. I have a grazing table set up in the sitting room. You'll just love the view of the water. Follow me."

Mac fought the urge to roll his eyes. Grazing? Great, it got worse. They were livestock now.

He stayed behind as Sarah led Elle and Travis to the sitting room, hoping no one would notice nor care that he wasn't there.

Mac needed a break. He hadn't lost his temper, and he had gotten Elle and Travis to the lodge safely. His job was done for today. And as soon as Mac got these suitcases upstairs, he was heading home.

He had one foot on the staircase when heavy, irregular footsteps grew louder behind him.

"Hey, Mac. Can you help me for a minute?"

He turned to face his sister. "I was just about to take the bags up."

Sarah waved her arm. "Leave them. Will can do that later."

Mac set the suitcases down with a sigh. "And what exactly do you need my help with? I'm not familiar with how things are done here at the Disco Ball Lodge."

"Don't be an ass. Will worked really hard on it." Sarah waddled closer, lowering her voice. "Can you come build a fire? I really want to give them the full Alaskan experience, but I can't bend down like that anymore."

Mac groaned. So much for his plan to get the hell out of there. "Why can't Will do it?"

"He's in town picking up a few last-minute things for dinner."

Mac swallowed a laugh. Hopefully, Will was picking up food from the Buck if they were planning on dinner being edible. It might be the only restaurant in Darling, but they had good food and even better beer. Sarah wasn't much of a cook, and Mac had only ever seen Will make burgers.

Not that Mac did much better. He usually ate a cold dinner out of a can. But he wasn't trying to impress anyone either. "Give it a break, Sarah. They're on vacation. Let them relax."

She looked up at him with puppy dog eyes. "Please? I just want everything to be perfect. Then you don't have to do anything else until it's time for them to fly back."

He sighed. "Promise?"

"Of course." Sarah blinked at him innocently.

Mac looked up at the ceiling. Why did he get the feeling that his involvement with these guests was not going to be as minimal as Sarah suggested? "Fine. I'll make a fire. Just keep this moment in mind when you're choosing a name for the baby. Maverick is a good name for a boy *or* a girl."

He followed Sarah to the sitting room, where she had set up a table covered in all sorts of bite-sized snacks. Sprigs of fresh spruce dotted the table. And a bottle of champagne chilled in a bucket, flanked by sparkling crystal glasses.

His eyebrows shot up his forehead. Where did Sarah even find a champagne bucket on the island?

The only normal thing about the whole setup was Bart snoozing on his dog bed in the corner. The little guy had a bed in every room in the lodge and always loved to be where the people were.

Sarah had called Mac a softie when he had bought all those dog beds in Ketchikan. Mac had taken offense. He wasn't a softie. Dogs were just easy to love.

Mac stooped to scratch Bart behind the ears, whispering to the dog, "Happy to see you aren't dyed hot pink and rolled in glitter."

While he stacked up kindling in the fireplace, Sarah chatted with Elle and Travis. "My husband, Will, is so excited to meet you both. He's in town right now, picking up a few things for dinner, but he'll be back soon."

"I hope you aren't going to too much trouble on our account," Elle said. "We don't need anything special."

"It's fine." Sarah waved her hand. "We do this for every guest."

Mac chuckled, pounding his chest with his fist as he turned it into a cough. Hopefully, that sounded convincing. He was choking on all this bullshit.

After the kindling got going, Mac laid a couple of logs across the top. He stood, dusting his hands. "Should be good to go with the fire, but I'll stick around a minute to make sure. Any of that champagne left?"

Sarah gave him a patient smile. "I'll pour you a glass while you wash your hands."

Mac opened his mouth to tell Sarah just exactly how he felt about being treated like a child when she shot him a look.

He snapped his mouth shut. Right. His best behavior. A promise he regretted more with each passing minute.

By the time he came back from washing his hands, the fire was roaring. Mac moved the wood around with a poker, holding his hands up afterwards to prove to Sarah they were still mostly clean.

She handed him his champagne, and Mac peered into the flute. "Any chance I get a full glass?"

Sarah smiled sweetly. "Don't you have to drive back to town soon?"

He worked his jaw. First, she asked him to help; now, she wanted him gone? Fine by him. The sooner he got out of here, the better. "I guess you're right."

Elle cleared her throat. "So you don't live at the lodge, Mac?"

Mac took a swig of his drink, trying not to take it personally that she sounded so relieved at that little realization. "Nope."

Sarah chuckled. "We had enough time together growing up."

"You've known each other a long time, then." Elle looked between the two of them.

Sarah added a few cubes of cheese to her plate. "My whole life. He's my brother."

Elle's face strained despite her small smile. "That's nice."

Based on her whiny tone, Mac was guessing *nice* wasn't the word she wanted to use.

Travis set down his empty champagne glass and reached for another smoked salmon and cream cheese sandwich. "These are so good."

Sarah beamed. "That's quite the compliment coming from a man who's practically married to a professional chef."

Elle picked up Travis's champagne glass, refilling it. "Chef is generous, but thank you."

Mac lifted an eyebrow. Now, that was good service. The guy didn't even have to ask.

He set down his glass. Alrighty. It was time to get out of here before Mac broke his good streak and actually spoke his mind. "I'll be by tomorrow with the rest of the stuff."

Sarah frowned. "What stuff?"

Mac shrugged. "We couldn't fit all her work crap in the plane. I mean, work stuff."

Sarah's face lit up, and she looked back at Elle. "Would you like me to set up one of the rooms as a workspace for you? We have a few empty."

Mac let out a huff. That was putting it mildly. Elle and Travis were the only two people here. How long did Sarah think it would take them to figure that out?

Elle glanced at Travis before looking back at Sarah. "That's so sweet of you. But I'm trying to take a break from posting this week and just focus on being on vacation."

Sarah's face fell ever so slightly, and Mac bit the inside of his cheek to keep from saying *I told you so*. Expecting anything from other people was a recipe for disappointment. "Right. Of course."

"Thanks anyway." Elle twisted her hands. "On that note, do you mind keeping the whole social media thing to yourself? This is our first vacation in a while, and we really just want to enjoy it."

"Absolutely." Sarah nodded, having recovered her composure for the most part. "Trust me, even if everyone in town knew, it wouldn't change a thing. None of that stuff matters here."

It was the truth, but based on the pinched look on Elle's face, she didn't look convinced.

Whatever. Elle's feelings weren't Mac's problem.

He waved over his shoulder and headed outside before Sarah roped him into something else. He had enough together time to last him a while.

Mac definitely didn't plan on hanging around when he dropped off Elle's work crap tomorrow. Hell, he might just slow down to five miles per hour and toss the bags out of the truck. Then Mac was going to spend the rest of the week avoiding the lodge.

The next time he saw Elle and Travis would be to take them home.

CHAPTER SIX

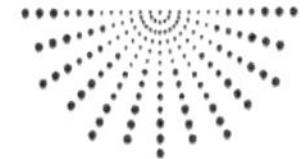

MAC

Mac stretched out his legs, glad to have the truck back to himself. The cab wasn't meant for three people, that's for damn sure.

Elle had sat in the middle since she was the smallest. But not so small that her toned leg hadn't spent the entire drive pressed into Mac's own, no matter how far he had scooted to the left.

He rubbed his thigh. Damn woman was obnoxious.

Elle was strictly off-limits. Even if she wasn't engaged, she wasn't his type. Every little thing seemed to stress her out. Why bother to go on vacation if she couldn't even relax?

The good news about that was that it was only a matter of time before her personality killed any and all attraction. All Mac had to do was keep his distance and wait it out.

He sighed. This had to be a sign of the times. It must have been at least a year and change since he'd been with a woman. Mac would have to get over to Juneau or Ketchikan one day soon and see if there wasn't some barfly that could scratch his itch. He had to make a trip for a new alternator anyway. Might as well multitask.

Mac glimpsed himself in the side mirror and muttered a curse. He snatched the hat off his head, flinging it onto the floor of the cab. He was never wearing the damn thing again, and it'd be a long time before he made any more promises.

Birch trees passed by in a black-and-white blur as he drove towards town. Mac chewed the inside of his cheek as he toyed with the idea of calling in a favor for Elle's return flight. That way, he'd never have to see her again after tomorrow.

But Mac quickly trashed the idea. Better to fly her out himself. He'd rest easier knowing beyond a shadow of a doubt that Elle was back in the lower forty-eight and far away from him. Something about her just *bugged* him.

He had stared down bears and winter sea storms and flight conditions that had suddenly turned sour. Mac did it all with ice water in his veins. The fact that Elle had gotten more of a reaction out of him didn't sit well.

As his shop came into view, Mac tightened his grip on the steering wheel and drove right past it. He had one more stop to make before calling it a night. A day like today called for more than a sip of bubbly wine.

Mac drove the rest of the way into town, parking in front of the Buckwild Bar and Grill. Everybody in Darling had been at the Buck at one time or another. It was the only watering hole that had survived the natural exodus of people who eventually left Alaska when the winters got too dark and too long. Not that there hadn't been other hopefuls. A deli, a pizza place, a bakery, to name a few.

He glanced across the street at the Driftwood Coffee Company, the *Open* sign flicked off. Until Grace had moved to town earlier this year and changed all their mornings for the better, the Buck was the one and only option in Darling for libations outside of a person's own home.

Pushing open the door to the restaurant, Mac inhaled the scent of home brew and fried food. His shoulders relaxed more with each step he took towards the bar. He hadn't met a problem yet that a beer or two couldn't fix. And that included irritating blondes from California.

Charlotte smiled at him from behind the counter. "Mac, honey. Did you want your usual? A growler to go?" Even though she'd lived in Darling for decades, her German accent hadn't completely faded away.

Mac scratched at his beard, trying to remember the last time he'd actually stayed at the bar. Most of the time, he preferred to drink alone at home. "Actually, I think I'm going to enjoy a drink here with you."

"I'm always happy for your company." Charlotte grabbed a pint glass and held it under the tap. "You've been keeping busy. I hear your plane all the time."

Mac nodded. "Trying to catch up. You know how slow winter is. Always feast or famine around here."

Charlotte placed the pint in front of him with a wink. "Speak for yourself. We do our best business in winter. Drinking is one of the few things to do."

Mac took a gulp, the bitter brew setting him right. "Remind me to ask Wolfie about that the next time I see him. I'm sure he'd have a thing or two to say about it."

Charlotte's husband and the co-owner of the Buck had worked as a psychologist in Germany before he traded it in for running a bar in Alaska. Mac had long suspected that the subjects on the island were more interesting than any Wolfie had encountered in his former career.

She smiled. "Well, that won't be today. Wolfie is over in Sitka. A brewery out there is selling off some older equipment, which means we're getting a new kettle."

Mac cocked his head. "More beer? You sure this town doesn't have a drinking problem?"

Charlotte lifted her hands in the air. "We had a decent crowd last summer, and we're expecting even more people this year. The coffee shop is open now, and soon, there may be more new additions to town." She looked him in the eye. "I've seen places revived from the dead before. You mark my words. Darling is growing."

He set down his glass and ran a hand over his mouth, careful to wipe away any foam. Not much he could say to that.

Mac didn't know Charlotte's whole story, and he didn't ask. Privacy was a right, in his opinion. But he knew from more than one drunken night with Wolfie that he and Charlotte had lived through the Berlin Wall coming up and going down. Mac could only imagine everything they'd seen in between, including a city coming back to life. "Even if you're right, I sure as hell don't like it. I don't want someone coming here to open a restaurant that serves nothing but broth. That's hippie crap."

Charlotte laughed. "Where did you get that idea?"

"Heard about it from a passenger. They have something like that in Seattle." He grimaced.

She lifted a shoulder. "Maybe this old lady would like some broth once in a while."

"I'll make you some damn broth." Mac drained his glass. One drink had been far from enough. "I think I will take a growler for the road. And a burger with extra onion rings, please."

She peered at him. "Tell me, am I imagining things, or are you a little more pokey than normal today?"

"More pokey?" He barked a laugh. "I'd say I'm at about my normal level of pokey."

Charlotte grabbed a growler from under the counter,

twisting off the cap. "Wolfie might have the degree, but I know people. Something is different."

Mac cracked his neck. "Nothing bad. Just an annoying passenger."

Charlotte gave him a knowing look. "A woman, I'm guessing?"

"Yep." Mac narrowed his eyes. "And don't look so smug. It's not what you think."

Her lips twitched. "It isn't?"

"For one, she's engaged. For two, that doesn't even matter. She's annoying as hell." He sighed, resting his hand on the bar. "Apparently, this lady is famous online or something, and Sarah is making a big deal about her being here. My sister seems to think if Elle posts about Darling, we'll have more business than we know what to do with."

Charlotte capped the growler and set it in front of him with a thump. "And you hate that idea."

"Like I said, I like this place exactly like it is." Mac tugged on his beard. "Not to mention, Sarah has been riding my ass about how to do my job on top of it."

"Language," Charlotte warned him.

Mac smacked the bar top. "Dammit, this is the last frontier. If a man can't talk freely here, then where can he?"

She raised a graying eyebrow.

"Fine." Mac mumbled an apology.

Charlotte gave him a sympathetic smile. "Sounds like you've had a hard day. How about I throw in a piece of chocolate mousse pie to help cheer you up?"

Mac grinned. "Remind me to complain more often."

Charlotte walked back towards the kitchen, pausing in the doorway. "Timing is interesting, isn't it?"

He squinted. "What do you mean?"

"There was an engagement in the way with me and Wolfie way back when."

Mac wrinkled his forehead. There was a part of the story he had never heard. "He was engaged?"

Charlotte shook her head. "No, honey. I was."

His eyes grew wide as Charlotte walked away, her petite form disappearing behind the swinging doors that went back to the kitchen. Charlotte, engaged? He'd never wanted to know their story so bad. But he had a feeling he'd have to wonder all his life.

Mac rolled the empty glass between his palms. Didn't matter anyway. Charlotte was missing the point. Mac didn't give a rat's ass if Elle was engaged or not. He wasn't interested in her like that.

If he was pokey, it was because this little interaction had only validated all the thoughts he had on women before. None of them could deal with his way of life. And it seemed he couldn't deal with them either.

His mind wandered back to the three of them stuffed in his truck cab, and Mac's thigh felt warm again.

Goddammit. He had to get out of town soon.

CHAPTER SEVEN

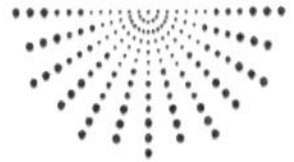

ELLE

The only thing worse than waking up in Alaska was waking
up in Alaska after not sleeping all night.

Elle set her phone down on the bedside table after
checking the time. At least she was one day closer to being
home.

She rested her head back on the pillow, her eyes gritty.
Despite being exhausted after the long day of travel, Elle had
tossed and turned the entire night. She wasn't used to
sharing a bed with Travis anymore, and she couldn't seem to
get comfortable no matter what she did.

Elle chewed her bottom lip. If she got up now, she'd probably have time to check her email before Travis was awake.
He was still breathing deeply beside her.

Her stomach twisted with guilt. Shouldn't she be able to
sleep in the same bed as her fiancé? But they hadn't shared a
bed in months. And even though she'd never tell Travis, she
didn't miss it.

Elle inched out from under the warm covers, one limb

at a time. She shivered in the cool morning air as she changed out of her pajamas. LA had mild weather year-round, and it had been years since Elle had woken up to a cold house.

Her throat tightened. Not since she left home.

Elle shoved the memory to the bottom of her mind and tiptoed out of the room. She needed to get to work. Once she started working, she'd be too busy for memories.

She stepped lightly down the hallway. Elle hadn't seen another guest yet, but everyone had to be sleeping right now. Most normal people were.

Elle made her way to the kitchen. She'd grab a cup of coffee and work until Travis woke up. Then, she would go back into vacation mode.

A crash came from the kitchen, and Elle froze. What was that? A bear? Or did someone break in?

Her heart pounded. The bear seemed more likely. There probably wasn't much crime in a town the size of a blueberry.

She inched closer to the kitchen, holding her breath as she peeked around the corner.

Elle's shoulders sagged. It wasn't a bear or a break-in. Just a very pregnant woman.

Sarah squatted awkwardly, grasping for a sheet pan that lay on the floor. The little dog, Bart, circled her.

Elle walked into the kitchen, clearing her throat. The last thing she wanted to do was startle Sarah. It seemed like the woman was having a hard enough morning. "Here, let me help you."

Sarah squeaked and snapped her head up. "I am so sorry. I didn't mean to wake you up." She breathed heavily. "This belly makes everything harder."

"I was already awake and on the hunt for coffee." Elle gave her a reassuring smile as she picked up the sheet pan.

"Can I pitch in with breakfast? I'm pretty good at cooking, or so I've been told."

Sarah shook her head. "Absolutely not. You're here on vacation."

"But I want to help." Elle placed her hands on her hips. "First things first. Where is the coffee?"

"Apparently, there's no stopping you." Sarah sighed and pointed to a cabinet. "The coffee is in there."

Elle grinned. "You should see me once I have caffeine."

She found the coffee tin and scooped up enough grounds for a full pot. She couldn't be the only one here who drank coffee.

Elle started the machine with a beep before opening the fridge. She inspected what she had to work with before turning to look at Sarah. "I've totally got this. Why don't you go back to bed and relax for a bit?"

Sarah perched on a stool at the kitchen island. "If you don't mind, I'd rather hang out with you. I can't remember the last time I had a conversation with someone besides Will or my brother." Her mouth quirked up at the corner. "Not that Mac is very chatty."

At the mention of Mac's name, Elle's skin tingled where his muscled arm had wrapped around her waist. She shook it off. She was tired and uncaffeinated. End of story. "He's definitely a man of few words."

Sarah's eyes narrowed. "He wasn't rude to you or anything, was he?"

Elle bit the inside of her cheek. Mac wasn't exactly warm and fuzzy, but he had gotten them to the lodge safely. That's all that mattered at the end of the day. "He was fine."

"Good. He can be a bit rough around the edges, but he had promised to be on his best behavior." Sarah coughed. "With all our guests."

Elle lifted an eyebrow. That was Mac's best behavior?

She'd hate to see him on a bad day. "Let me get you something else to drink since I'm assuming coffee is off the table."

Searching through the cabinets, Elle found the glasses and poured Sarah some orange juice.

Sarah accepted the glass. "Okay, now you're really making me feel guilty. I should be waiting on you."

"I'm not about to have a baby." Elle found the cabinet with the pots and pans. She grabbed a cast-iron skillet and started it heating on the stove. "Although eating for two sounds like fun."

"You'll get to do it one day," Sarah said confidently.

Elle's stomach tightened. It's not that she didn't want kids. But she was afraid to take on one more responsibility. Afraid the house of cards would fall. Afraid Travis wasn't the one for her.

Guilt stabbed at her stomach. Not to mention, sharing a bed was kind of a requirement for having kids.

The coffee maker beeped, and Elle's shoulders sagged. Saved by the bell.

She poured herself a cup, her mouth watering at the scent of freshly brewed coffee. "This is even better than champagne."

Sarah laughed. "If you change your mind, I have the makings for mimosas."

Elle lifted an eyebrow. Maybe Travis's friend hadn't been completely wrong about this place. It definitely wasn't her first pick for a vacation, but it had more perks than she had expected. "No wonder people love it here. You make it hard not to."

"I'm so glad to hear that." Sarah beamed. "Will and I worked really hard to make this place great. I wouldn't be in Darling without him. I doubt the lodge would be in business at all."

Elle set her coffee aside and grabbed a package of bacon from the fridge. "Is Will from here too?"

Last night at dinner, Sarah had peppered her with questions. Elle hadn't had a chance to learn much about her hosts yet.

"He's from Seattle. I had hired him to help at the lodge, and that's how we met." Sarah took another sip of orange juice. "Although at the time, I didn't realize he had a wife."

Elle's jaw dropped. It was clear from the moment she had met Will that he adored Sarah. Elle couldn't imagine him with anyone else. "Seriously?"

"My thoughts exactly." Sarah shook her head. "Later, I found out that he had taken the job at the lodge to get away from a messy divorce."

Elle sliced the bacon and added it to the skillet with a sizzle. "And then what happened?"

While Elle diced vegetables and cracked eggs, Sarah told her all about Will's first summer at the Salmonberry Lodge. Even though the situation had been complicated, it was clear that Will and Sarah were head over heels for each other.

Elle took a sip of her coffee, but the lump in her throat didn't move. Some people had love like that. So what if she wasn't one of them? She didn't even want it.

She slid the frittata into the oven and set the timer. "Breakfast should be done in about twenty minutes."

Sarah gaped at her. "Oh my God, I've been talking your ear off the whole time you've been working. I'm the worst."

"No, you're not." Elle shook her head. "I enjoyed it. Really."

She meant it. It had been so long since Elle had cooked a meal that didn't end with taking fifty photos just to get the perfect one that it took her a minute to realize what this strange feeling was.

She was actually having fun.

Elle pulled her phone from her pocket. "But if you don't mind, I'm going to check on a few things while I wait for the frittata to bake."

She squinted at her phone, surprised to see it was still on airplane mode. Normally, she never turned it off, but she was determined to do everything she could to make this vacation great for Travis. Elle tapped on the screen, and the phone beeped nonstop as one message after another came in.

"Holy crap, that's a lot of messages." Sarah's face crumbled. "I really am the worst."

Elle frowned. "What do you mean? You didn't have anything to do with this. It's just a normal day for me."

Sarah's cheeks turned red. "The thing is, I had been hoping you'd post about the lodge." She gestured to Elle's phone. "It was selfish. You're already buried in work, and this is supposed to be your vacation. I'm so embarrassed to admit I even had the idea in the first place."

Elle's stomach sank. Everything made a lot more sense. Sarah offering to set up a workspace for Elle. Mac being on his best behavior. The champagne yesterday and mimosas for breakfast today. Plus the fact that Travis's friend hadn't mentioned any of these perks because he probably didn't have them.

She should be used to this by now. Grateful, even. People bought her opinion because it mattered. It was a good problem in her line of work.

But some teeny-tiny part of her wished that for just one day, she could be enough on her own, without the followers and the likes and reposts. "There's nothing for you to feel bad about. After all, that's my job."

"Still, I wish there was some way I could make it up to you. But it seems the best thing I can do right now is to leave you alone finally." Sarah climbed off the stool. "At least you have the picnic hike to look forward to. Will takes you to this great spot right on the water."

Elle forced a smile. "I can't wait." Travis was excited about the hike. That meant she would be excited about it too. "Will there be other people on the hike or just us?"

Sarah glanced away. "There, uh, aren't any other guests at the lodge right now."

Elle's heart squeezed as the pieces fell into place. So that's why Sarah had wanted Elle to post. She wasn't just hungry for exposure. The lodge was struggling for business. But Sarah had too much pride to ask for help outright. That was something Elle could understand.

"I'll post about the lodge, okay? I promise. That will definitely get this place some attention." She gave Sarah a reassuring smile. "I'm sure we'll get great pictures from the hike today."

Elle had expected Sarah to be happy, but instead, her face strained. "That's really nice of you. Really. But the truth is—"

A loud noise sounded overhead, and Sarah looked up. "I think that's coming from my room. I have to go."

Sarah waddled out of the kitchen, and Bart jumped up from his dog bed to follow her.

Elle bit her lip. Should she go with Sarah? Elle checked the timer on the frittata. It wasn't very helpful to make breakfast if she was just going to burn it. Once that was done, she'd see if Sarah needed her.

With her coffee cup in hand, Elle made her way into the sitting room. She settled onto the goose-down sofa that faced the window. Outside, dawn lit up the Alaskan landscape with a warm glow.

Sarah hadn't been lying yesterday when she said the view was incredible.

Thick trees framed the window, blurring the line between inside and outside. The ocean sparkled like a sapphire in the early morning sun. And dark mountains poked their heads up in the distance.

All the views back home were of the city skyline, other buildings, and other people. This felt almost prehistoric by comparison.

It would make for great photos. As much as Elle didn't want to be here in the first place, posting about her Alaskan vacation would both keep her manager happy *and* help Sarah. It would also send the message to Travis that she was having a good time.

She shifted on the couch. Sarah wasn't the worst. Elle was. She shouldn't have to make a conscious effort to convince her fiancé that she was having a good time.

Suddenly chilled, Elle set her coffee on the side table and pulled a throw blanket across her knees. Too bad Mac wasn't here to build a fire again.

Elle made a face. She had not just thought that. Gross.

She grabbed her phone and buried herself in her emails, hoping the combination of work and caffeine would get her head on straight.

Only a few minutes later, the timer beeped for the frittata. Elle stood with a sigh and headed back to the kitchen.

As she set the frittata on a trivet to cool, Sarah waddled back into the room. "Everything okay?"

Sarah twisted her hands. "Elle, I'm so sorry. We have a problem."

CHAPTER EIGHT

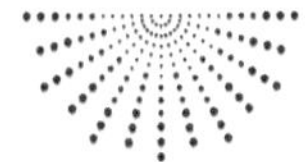

MAC

Mac pushed open the door to the Driftwood Coffee Company, going weak in the knees at the scent of freshly brewed coffee. It was a far cry from the plastic tub he scooped coffee from at home.

Grace gaped at him from where she stood behind the counter. "Am I losing it? I don't think I've ever seen you in here after the sun was up."

Mac sighed. If he wasn't the first customer of the day, he didn't bother coming into the coffee shop at all. He got up early as it was, and coming in first thing gave him the best chance of avoiding people. "Long day. Night. Whatever."

He had left town at first light, going to get Elle's things from Ketchikan. Which wasn't easy, having finished off the growler the night before.

But Mac had wanted that errand off his mind. It was all that stood between him and being done with the lodge, and Elle, for the rest of the week.

He should've gone straight to the lodge as soon as he was

back in Darling. But Mac had needed a pick-me-up. All it had taken was one sip of crappy coffee from his ancient drip pot to send him straight to the Driftwood.

Grace's lips twitched. "Sounds like it."

Mac handed her the ceramic mug he had brought with him. "Can I get my usual?"

She nodded, setting the cup in the dish bin behind the counter.

While Grace started his pour-over, her miniature Australian shepherd, Ruby, pranced over to greet Mac.

Mac bent down and scratched the dog's soft ears. Maybe he should get a dog. That was probably the closest he'd ever get to someone being happy to see him at the end of the day.

His shoulders sagged. No, that wouldn't work either. It wasn't fair to leave a dog home alone all day while he flew all over southeast Alaska.

Mac straightened and glanced at the bookshelves that lined the wall. "Get any new books in recently?"

Grace had practically brought a library with her when she moved to Darling. The collection was constantly changing as people borrowed and donated books. The whole thing ran on an honor system. For a reader like Mac, it was heaven.

She looked up. "I actually got a few this morning. Did you want to look through them?"

Mac rubbed the back of his neck. Tempting. But the sooner he got this errand over with, the better. "Maybe next time. I have to take some luggage out to the lodge right now."

Grace poured the freshly brewed coffee into a clean ceramic mug and handed it to Mac. Reusable cups were less wasteful than disposable ones. Those ran on an honor system too. "I'm surprised Sarah still has people there."

"Don't get me started." He took a small sip, savoring the rich brew. Mac used to think people who bought coffee instead of making it at home were lazy. Now he knew the difference. They had taste buds. "Damn. That's good."

She laughed. "I'll never get used to Darling. You all are so easy to please."

He frowned. "You thinking of leaving us?"

As much as he hated change, he was okay with the addition of the coffee shop to town. Besides good coffee and books, he liked Grace. She didn't gossip, she was almost as private as he was, and she had made it clear from day one that she was in no way, shape, or form interested in dating. All anyone knew was that she was divorced, and she wanted to stay that way.

Grace shook her head. "Never. I've seen enough of the world to know this is home. That's all I've ever wanted."

Mac took another sip of coffee. "What's so different about Darling?"

Grace cocked her head. "Different from what? Where I lived before?"

Mac nodded. "Yeah. From your old home."

She blew air through her lips. "Hard to compare it to my old home when I didn't really have one. My ex's work kept us on the move. I was too busy to think. That's probably why it took me so long to figure out that wasn't the life for me."

He scratched his beard, glancing out the window as a truck rumbled by. Grace was at least a few years older than him. She must have lived a full life before Darling. "Bet you think this place is boring."

Grace shrugged. "At first, it felt a little slow. Once I got things off the ground with the coffee shop, that wasn't a problem anymore."

His phone rang, and Mac slipped it from his pocket. "Sorry, gotta take this." He tapped on the screen. "Hey, Sarah. I already got Elle's stuff from Ketchikan and am back in town. I'll head out to the lodge soon."

"That's great."

His shoulders tensed at her tone. "Out with it."

She sighed. "I need another favor."

He turned his back to Grace, lowering his voice. No need to air their dirty laundry right in the middle of the Driftwood Coffee Company, even if Grace wasn't a gossip. "I thought that me putting a smile on my face was all you needed. Then it was social hour. Remember the part when you told me that would be the end of it?"

"Please," she begged. "Will has some kind of stomach bug, and he can't take Elle and Travis on the picnic hike. So I was hoping you could."

Mac gritted his teeth. This was in direct opposition to the plan to not involve himself with the lodge until it was time for Elle to go home. But he couldn't very well expect Sarah to go traipsing around the forest in her condition. Still, there had to be another option. "Maybe they don't even want to go. They're probably tired from yesterday."

"We need this, Mac."

He cracked his neck. It was only a year ago Mac had asked the same thing of Sarah. If she hadn't said yes, the Salmonberry Lodge might be history by now. It was a reminder of how far they'd come. And how much they had to lose. "I'll be there within half an hour. But I swear to God, no more special requests."

Sarah squealed. "Thank you, thank you, thank you! Best uncle ever!"

He smiled despite the unwelcome change to his plans. "Just make sure the kid knows that."

Mac shoved the phone back in his pocket and turned to Grace. He lifted the coffee cup. "See you next time. I'm headed out to the lodge."

Grace smirked. "Try not to have too much fun."

"Not a snowball's chance in hell."

CHAPTER NINE

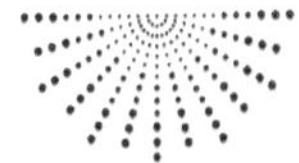

ELLE

"Are you sure you don't mind?"

Travis smiled. "Of course not. I'm just happy to be here with you."

Elle nodded, her stomach churning with a mix of guilt at disappointing Travis and the relief of not having to go on the hike.

She was an awful person. That was the only explanation.

Elle picked up the coffeepot, refilling his cup. She couldn't control the fact that Will was sick or that work was piling up or that she was exhausted. But she could control her attitude. "What do you want to do instead? We could walk down to the water and take some photos." She shook her head. "Never mind. I can do that another time."

Travis scooped up another bite of frittata. "I understand that you have to work, babe."

Elle smiled. Nope. She didn't deserve a guy like Travis. "Maybe Sarah can give us a ride to check out the town later on."

Which would probably take all of ten minutes, but Elle didn't have any other ideas of how to fill their day.

Travis sipped his coffee. "We could talk about the wedding."

Elle's smile froze on her face. She had no doubt about it now. She was definitely screwed up. A great, handsome, kind man wanted to marry her, and she dreaded talking about it.

But he was right. They needed to get started. Weddings already took an immense amount of planning, and marrying Los Angeles royalty was even more of a production. "Great idea. I'll go get ready for a walk while you finish up here."

Elle pressed a kiss to his forehead and went to get changed. As she passed by the entryway, the front door swung open, and Mac stepped inside.

She cringed. Shoot. She'd rather go on the hike than deal with him. "What are you doing here?"

"Good morning to you too." Mac stomped his feet on the shoe mat. "I brought all your crap from Ketchikan."

Elle swallowed. It was a little thing. It shouldn't mean so much. Mac had said he would bring her stuff, and he did.

But Elle was so used to relying on herself for everything. When was the last time she actually let someone help her, whether or not she wanted to? "Thank you."

"No problem," he grunted.

"Did he tell you the good news?" a voice called out behind her.

Elle turned to see Sarah grinning as she picked her way down the stairs. "Good news?"

Sarah walked over to them, breathing heavily. "Mac can take you on the hike. He was on his way here anyway. It worked out perfectly."

Perfectly wasn't the word Elle would use. And based on the pained expressed on Mac's face, she guessed he felt the same way. "It's fine, really. You don't have to do that."

"It's a family business. And I'm family." Mac bared his teeth in what Elle assumed was supposed to be a smile. "You ready?"

She blinked. "Now?"

He nodded. "Yep. I sure as hell don't want to be out there in the dark. Do you?"

"Mac," Sarah said in a warning tone. "There's no rush."

The only rush Elle was in was trying to figure a way out of this. But even as her mind raced through every possible excuse, she already knew exactly what she would do. Because Elle always did what she should do, not what she wanted. Right now, that meant making Travis happy. That's what he deserved. "That's very nice of you."

Mac gave a firm nod and turned to Sarah. "The city slicker feeling better?"

Sarah let out a sigh. "Yes, thank goodness. He's finally resting. I don't know what kind of witchcraft Elle did in the kitchen, but she threw together a tea that settled his stomach."

Mac raised an eyebrow. "Witchcraft, huh?"

Elle would bet her entire social media following on the fact that Mac thought she was an actual witch.

He smiled at her. He never raised his voice. He had brought her stuff like he promised. But Elle couldn't shake the feeling that he didn't like her any more than she liked him.

Mac looked between Sarah and Elle. "Seems like you two are getting along."

Sarah beamed at Elle. "She's the absolute best. We should be paying her to be here, not the other way around."

"I'm having a great time." Elle gave Sarah a reassuring smile.

Mac looked at Elle. "And your lap dog?"

"My what?" she asked with a frown.

Sarah looked confused. "Are you talking about Bart?"

Mac shook his head. "Not *your* lap dog." His gaze locked on Elle. "*Your* lap dog."

Was he insulting Travis? "I don't know what you're talking about."

"Sure you do. About this tall." Mac held his hand just below his shoulder. "Answers to the name Travis."

"Mac," Sarah hissed. "Cut it out."

The room felt too hot, too small. Just like she had thought—Mac was no fan of hers. Elle clenched her fists, driving her nails into her palms. She and Travis might not be head over heels for each other, but at least he wasn't a jerk like the man in front of her.

Mac held her gaze, his mouth quirked up. But Elle wouldn't give him the satisfaction of reacting. This was about Travis. In a week, Mac would be out of her life forever. Elle wouldn't lose focus of what mattered. "Are we going or what?"

Sarah crossed her arms, giving Mac a pointed look. "You promised, remember?"

His jaw tensed. "Of course."

Elle bit back a smile. Thanks to Sarah's chatting, Elle knew that Mac was all bark and no bite. But he didn't know that she knew that.

Travis walked into the room. "Hey, Mac. What's going on?"

Elle clapped her hands together. She refused to let whatever problem Mac had with her affect Travis's vacation. "Good news. We can go on that hike after all."

Travis's face lit up. "Cool. Glad it worked out."

Elle smiled at him. Mac might fly a plane and chop wood or whatever, but Travis was more of a man than Mac would ever be. And as soon as they got back from the hike, they would set a date for the wedding.

CHAPTER TEN

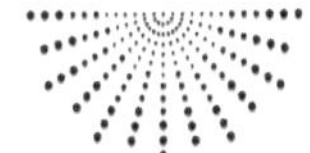

ELLE

Elle hated this stupid forest. She hated this stupid wilderness, island, state. Whatever a person wanted to call it. But most of all, she hated Maverick Carter.

She lagged behind Mac and Travis. Elle wasn't trying to keep up anymore. At this point, she had settled for not losing sight of them altogether.

If it wasn't for stopping to take photos, Elle would've collapsed an hour ago.

Her legs felt heavier with each step. The backpack straps dug into her shoulders. And even though the trail seemed mostly flat, Elle would swear they had been going uphill the entire time.

But worst of all, every so often, Mac would look back at her with that smug look on his face and ask if she was doing alright.

Elle gave him a silent thumbs-up each time. It had to be obvious she was barely making it. But she had never admitted defeat before, and she certainly wasn't starting with Mac.

The one single thing that kept her going wasn't her love for Travis or the gritty determination that had driven her all these years. It was the fact that she knew no matter what, Mac had to be nice to her. Elle clung to that for all it was worth.

She sucked in a ragged breath as she plodded up the trail. This would be so much easier if she wasn't completely out of shape.

Elle kept her figure by keeping busy. There were days when the only bite of food she ate was in front of the camera. She didn't have time to go to the gym. She didn't have time for anything but work.

Travis, on the other hand, had no trouble keeping up with Mac. Not that it surprised her. Travis spent his days working out, playing sports, and surfing. He was in great shape.

He looked back at Elle with a grin. "Isn't this gorgeous? It's so green. I don't think we've had this much rain in California in the last ten years combined."

Elle wiped her hair away from her forehead, pushing the damp waves back. She wasn't quite enjoying the experience with the same wide-eyed wonder. Elle was more focused on the blister forming on her ankle from her socks soaking up all that great Alaskan rain. "They definitely don't have a drought."

She continued to trudge along, staying quiet rather than complaining. With each step, she felt more and more like the ancient family mule with one foot in the grave. It would be more merciful to cut her loose.

Back by herself, the softly falling mist and spongy forest floor wrapped her in silence. Elle wasn't sure she liked it. In LA, there was always background noise. Here, there was nothing.

She lifted her gaze from the trail at the sound of stomping boots.

Elle swallowed, glancing up ahead to make sure Travis was out of earshot. "Tell me this is almost over."

Mac's mouth twisted into a pathetic excuse for a smile. "It's not. I came back here to make sure you're still alive. I've never seen someone have such a hard time with a literal picnic before."

"Picnic?" Elle gasped. "This isn't a picnic. I am pretty sure walking the Oregon Trail was easier."

Mac barked a laugh. "This trail is so easy that you'd have to be an idiot to get lost."

She didn't miss the quick glance he shot in Travis's direction. Her stomach churned with anger, driving the chill from her body. "Is this what you consider your best behavior?

Mac gritted his teeth. "And what would you know about that?"

"Why don't we ask Sarah?" she said sweetly.

He tugged at his beard. "Fine. I'll slow down. Then we can all hike together like one big happy family. Is that what you'd prefer?"

She placed her hands on her hips, sticking her chin out. Elle hated conflict. Avoided it at all costs. She'd heard enough arguments between her parents to last her a lifetime. But something about Mac made her want to confront him head-on. "I'd prefer you weren't here at all."

Mac gave her the satisfaction of turning a particular shade of pink. Just when Elle was going to remind him to breathe, he broke his silence. "I definitely can't say no to the famous Elle Blessing. That wouldn't be very nice of me, would it?"

He pointed to the ground. "Let me give you a quick tutorial. See that dirt? That's the trail. This is an island, so if you get lost, the ocean is a good point of reference. Any questions?"

She swallowed, her anger replaced with doubt. It was one thing to put Mac in his place. But this was the wilderness. No amount of self-righteousness would save her out here. "Get lost?"

Mac lifted an eyebrow, a smug look passing across his face. "Having a change of heart?"

Elle shook her head. She'd rather get lost than give this goon the satisfaction of admitting she needed his help. "Nope. If anyone is going to get lost, it's you. Right now."

The power shifted again as color flooded back into Mac's face, peeking out over his beard. "Fine by me. I'll get lost. You better not." He leaned so close she could see the yellow and brown specks in his green eyes. "Either way, don't plan on seeing me again until it's time for you to go home."

Mac turned on his heel, his boot leaving a divot in the ground. As his khaki jacket disappeared into the trees, Elle's relief at seeing him leave was again replaced with the worry that maybe this hadn't been her best idea.

But no good ever came from looking back. She couldn't control what had already happened. Only what lay in front of her.

Elle plodded up the trail to where Travis waited. Her stomach was heavy with guilt. So far, his special trip wasn't turning out to be very special at all. But it was only their first full day in Alaska. There was still time for things to turn around. "Looks like we're finishing the hike by ourselves. Sorry."

"Nothing to be sorry about." Travis draped his arm across her shoulders. "We'll have more fun just the two of us anyway."

Travis pressed a kiss to her cheek before stepping away to take the lead.

Elle adjusted her backpack and followed behind him, her gaze glued to the trail.

Her fear of getting lost was matched only by her determination to prove she could do this. Mac had no idea just how strong she was, but Elle was about to show him.

After all, she wasn't an idiot.

CHAPTER ELEVEN

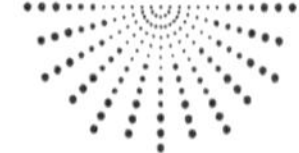

MAC

Mac set down his book, letting out a moan as he stretched his arms overhead.

After that disaster of a hike, he had decided to call it a day and go back to his shop. There, Mac had taken a hot shower, poured himself a glass of his favorite whisky, and settled into his leather chair to read.

He took another sip of the smoky liquor, smacking his lips. This was pretty close to heaven. All that was missing was a fireplace.

Mac scratched his beard. Maybe he should get a real home one of these days. The shop had been good enough all these years, but it was natural for a man to crave a castle.

He closed his eyes, trying to imagine it. A fireplace was a given, of course. Alaska nights were cool, even in summer. A bigger kitchen would be nice. And a real bathtub. Something wide and deep, not just a shower built for someone half his size.

Mac rubbed his chin. Did he want two or three bedrooms? Or four?

He snapped his eyes open, shaking his head. What the hell was he thinking? A single man did not need four bedrooms.

Just as he stood to refill his drink, his cell phone vibrated on the side table.

Mac squinted at it. No one ever called him this time of day. A last-minute flight for tomorrow, maybe?

As soon as he saw Sarah's name flashing across the screen, he answered. Hopefully, everything was okay with the baby. "What's going on?"

"Mac," she yelled into the phone. "Where the hell are you?"

He wrinkled his forehead. "I'm at my place."

"Are they with you?"

The hair on the back of his neck stood up. "They?"

"Elle and Travis. Are they with you? I haven't seen them since you left for the hike."

Shit.

A pounding started behind his eyes. There went his pleasant evening down the drain. "They said they would rather do the hike themselves. And you know that trail. You'd have to be—"

"An idiot to get lost," she finished for him. "Or someone who doesn't know this island. You're the idiot!"

A knock rang out on the door, and the pounding behind his eyes got worse. Mac rubbed his forehead with his free hand. "Hold on. Someone's here."

He set the phone down, still able to hear Sarah's tinny yelling as he walked away.

Mac rarely found himself surprised in life. Not tickled. Never delighted. But when he opened the door, he had the words sucked right out of him.

Elle stood in front of him, looking like she had been to

hell and back. Her hair was a frizzy mess, her face flushed. "Travis is gone."

Mac glanced over her head to Sarah's truck parked behind her. "Is that how you got here?"

Elle turned and followed his gaze before nodding. "The keys were in the ignition."

He sighed. "And you know where I live how?"

"I stopped and asked at the first place with lights on."

Mac shook his head. Damn town had no boundaries. "Give me a minute." He walked back to the side table and grabbed his phone. "Sarah, Elle is here. And so is your truck. Don't worry, I'll handle this. Take care of yourself and the baby."

She was still squealing when he hung up the phone, but Mac couldn't handle both women at once. Hell, he could barely handle one at a time.

When he turned back around, Elle was sitting in his chair. Mac swept his arms out. "Make yourself at home, why don't you?"

Her blue eyes were as cold as a glacier. "This is your fault."

Mac splayed his hand against his chest. "My fault? How is it my fault your lap dog is missing?"

She balled her small hands, the diamond glinting with the movement. "His name is *Travis*. He's not a dog. And he's lost."

"Sorry." The apology turned his mouth sour. In his opinion, the statute of limitations on his promise to Sarah had run its course. He had thought he was agreeing to his best behavior for two flights, not hourly activities. But he'd be damned if he broke his word, even if Elle made it next to impossible to keep his cool. "What happened exactly?"

Her forehead wrinkled. "I stopped to take a break. I thought—well, I thought I was going to be sick. Travis said he was going to explore a bit." Her voice grew quiet. "I stayed there for a while, and he never came back. Once it started to get dark, I had to come back before I got lost too."

Mac's back tensed. "Where exactly did he explore?"

She threw her hands in the air. "Off the trail somewhere. I don't know. If I did, I wouldn't be here."

He ran a hand through his hair. "Apparently, the California public education system hasn't added common sense to their curriculum."

"Apparently, neither has Alaska!" she yelled, jumping to her feet. "You're the one who left us out there."

"You seemed fine with it at the time!" he roared back.

Because of his size, people had always shrunk away from him. They reacted to his anger like they would to a German shepherd barking and baring his teeth. But not Elle. The blonde pixie leaned in, moving closer to the fire.

This was a woman who, for all intents and purposes, had stolen a truck and tracked him down on a moment's notice. Elle was the type who would be too busy doing something to be afraid.

He might not like her. But he was starting to think he could respect her.

"The point is he's lost. Or at least, we don't know where he is."

Elle sucked in rapid breaths. "He's lost. It's not like this is our neighborhood and he's at a friend's house somewhere."

Mac held up a finger, making his way to the cabinet. He grabbed the whisky, refilling his glass and getting a fresh one for Elle. "This won't help Travis, but I think we could use it."

She accepted the glass, and with the bravado he had only seen from sailors, hunters, and teenage boys, Elle threw back the drink.

Mac gaped at her. "That was good shit."

She narrowed her eyes, daring him to say more.

"Try to sip it this time." Mac tipped the bottle over her

glass again. "Here's the thing. We'll find the guy. It's an island, not LA. There's only so many places he can go, unless he's part merman or something. But we have to wait until tomorrow. It's dark outside, not to mention cold as shit. Better to rest now and start fresh in the morning."

Elle's small hands wrapped around the glass.

Small but mighty.

She looked him in the eye. "Here's the thing." Mac bristled as she used his own words against him. "I'm going to look for Travis tonight. With or without you."

Elle sat her unfinished glass down and walked away.

Mac watched her disappear through the doorway, a mix of rage and respect burning in his belly. He supposed it was a pleasant change from feeling nothing.

With a sigh, Mac set down his drink and went after her.

CHAPTER TWELVE

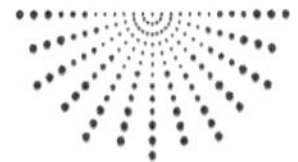

MAC

Mac swept the flashlight back and forth. He illuminated trees, bushes, and dirt, but no Travis. Just like he thought.

When he had followed Elle back out to the lodge in his truck, Mac had thought it would only take a few minutes of stomping through the pitch-black forest for her to realize how pointless it was. Which might have been the case if she wasn't the one person on Earth more stubborn than him.

"Travis!" She stumbled as she focused the flashlight ahead of her instead of down on the trail. "Travis!"

Mac made a mental note to remember this moment the next time he got the wild hair to shack up with someone. Instead of having a cozy evening with a good book, he was on a doomed mission with a woman who stole trucks and shot whisky straight. Definitely not what he expected when he first saw Elle. He thought she was more suited to being a model. He had been wrong.

"Look, Elle." Mac kept his voice calm. It was probably too late to make a good impression. But she was upset, and the last thing Mac wanted to do was make it worse. He wasn't sure he could handle worse. "We've been out here for two hours. If Travis could hear us, we'd have found him by now."

She shifted beside him, her rain jacket crinkling. "What if he has hypothermia?"

Mac stroked his beard, damp from the steady mist that fell from the night sky. "This time of year? No. It's pretty cold, but not cold enough for that. He was probably tired and hungry and decided to stop somewhere. Did he have a flashlight?"

"Not that I know of," she said quietly.

Mac sighed. "Okay, then I think we can safely assume he's not trying to find his way back right now. It's time to call it a night."

Her flashlight bobbed as she took a step forward. "We have to keep looking."

He clenched his jaw. "No. We've done our due diligence. Now, we are going back to get what little sleep we can. We will keep looking in the morning."

"Speak for yourself." The flashlight moved away from him at a clipped pace, Elle's voice hoarse as she yelled Travis's name.

Mac sucked in a deep breath. Right now, being on his best behavior meant not letting Elle hurt herself, whether she liked it or not. "Alright, that's enough negotiating."

He made his way to where Elle's flashlight shone. Mac reached out, finding her form, and picked her up.

Elle shrieked and pounded on his chest with her small fists. He let out a grunt as she got a good whack in with the flashlight. "Put me down! You go. I'm staying."

He kept walking in the direction of the lodge, one hand holding her to his shoulder and the other holding the flashlight. "We can't have two people go missing on us. That's just bad publicity."

Elle fought him all the way back, and the weirdest feeling came over Mac. Instead of being annoyed, a laugh bubbled up inside him. His life had followed the same routine since he was a teenager. Within a day of Elle arriving in Darling, he found himself carrying around a blonde at midnight and trying to find a missing person. It was so bizarre that it was almost comical. Not that he would let her know that.

They finally got back to the lodge, and Mac set her down on the front porch with a thud. "Now, go in there and close the door behind you. If you want to go keep looking by yourself, fine. But at least wait until you can't see my taillights so I can live in peaceful ignorance."

Elle stared up at him. In the reflection of the porch light, he could see the determination in her blue eyes. He saw the battle laid out in front of him. And he was ready.

But it seemed Elle would never stop surprising him.

Without a word, she went inside the lodge. Mac braced himself for the door to slam, but she closed it softly behind her.

His shoulders sagged with relief at her apparent self-control. No need to scare Sarah with a loud noise in the middle of the night, if she was even able to sleep after all this. His pregnant sister had been through enough for one day.

Mac got back into his truck, peeling out of the driveway the minute the engine roared to life. He didn't want to see Elle leave the lodge again. Mac wouldn't be able to just drive away if he did.

It wasn't that he was okay with Travis wandering off God knows where. Mac had a soul, after all. But he knew today's chance to look for him was gone.

Besides, they were both exhausted. Or at least Mac was. That's the only reason he couldn't stop thinking about how much he enjoyed holding Elle's body close to his for the second time in as many days.

Mac ran a hand over his face. He really was going stir-crazy. The most annoying woman on the planet came to him in the middle of the night to find her lost fiancé, and he felt aroused? What the hell was wrong with him?

He shifted in his seat. That's it. Once they found the lap dog tomorrow, Mac was going to get off the island for a day or two and get his head on straight. Then it would be time to take Elle home, and he'd never think about her again.

CHAPTER THIRTEEN

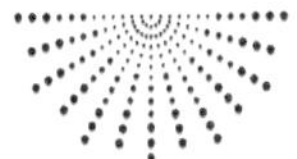

ELLE

She wasn't alone. A hand gripped her shoulder, and a familiar voice called her name. Elle peeled her eyes open, her head thick from lack of sleep and stress.

Elle sat up. All of it caused by the very man sitting on her bed.

The moonlight washed over his face, illuminating his serene smile. "Hey, babe."

"Travis," she croaked, her throat dry. "What the hell? We've been looking for you. I was worried sick." Elle blinked. "I stole a truck."

He chuckled. "You always were too good for me."

Were.

Elle latched onto that like the corner piece of a puzzle, the critical clue she needed. Suddenly, she was wide-awake. "What are you talking about? Take a shower and come to bed. We're both tired. You can tell me what happened in the morning."

He shook his head. "I won't be here in the morning."

She reached out, running her hands up and down his arms. "Why? Are you hurt?"

"I've never felt better." Travis took her hands and held them still. "I'll admit, when I couldn't find my way back to you, I was scared. But after a while, it's like the forest took care of me. For the first time in my life, I wasn't dependent on another person. This is where I belong, Elle."

She frowned. "Alaska?"

"Nature." He whispered the word with the kind of reverence reserved for religious artifacts. "For now, that's here. But there is an entire world of nature out there."

Her head swam as she tried to make sense of everything. "But...but you don't know the first thing about survival or the great outdoors or anything!"

A dreamy look passed across his face. "I know. I have so much to learn."

Elle jerked her hands free and cradled his face, peering into his eyes. "You didn't eat any berries, did you? Or mushrooms? Do mushrooms even grow here?"

He laughed with that annoying patience only saints were supposed to have. "I get it. It's a lot to take in. But I know you can handle explaining to everyone."

She knit her brows together. "Explain what?"

"About the wedding."

Elle dropped her hands, going from confused to sick in a moment. This wasn't happening. Without Travis, there was no Elle. "Don't do this. Please."

Travis reached out and plucked the ring from the nightstand, the giant diamond glinting like a star in the moonlight. "I want you to keep it."

She felt light-headed. "It's not just the wedding, Travis. What about my career? Our lives?" She scrambled for a way to make him understand. "What about your parents? You told me how happy they are that you're in a serious relationship. That you're finally getting your life together. That's why this works, Travis!"

"Elle, you don't want to marry me. Which is fine because I don't want to marry you." He set the ring down, his eyes rounded in apparent sympathy. "I can't keep living a lie just because it works. I'm not as strong as you."

Elle swallowed, her heart pounding. "What do you mean?"

He held her gaze. "I think it's pretty obvious you aren't happy."

The floor dropped out from under her. Elle had built a life on pretending. If Travis knew, did that mean everyone else did too? Were they all just pretending along with her?

Elle grabbed his hand. She had to fix this. She couldn't start over. Not again. "Travis, please. There has to be another way. We can still get married, and we can visit Alaska whenever you want."

He glanced away. "That's not going to work."

"Tell me." She squeezed his hand. "Tell me why that won't work."

"Because if I go back now, everything will stay the same. The time to make changes is when things are already different." He pulled his hand away and pressed a kiss to her forehead. "Goodbye, Elle. If you want to talk, you know where to find me."

Travis stood, and bile rose in the back of her throat. This wasn't happening. He wasn't leaving her.

She grabbed a pillow and then another, hurling them at the door as he walked out. "Sure! I'll just send a flipping carrier pigeon!"

Travis didn't even turn around.

Elle threw herself back on the mattress and kicked off the covers, her body hot. She didn't even want to come here in the first place. Now she had no fiancé. Probably no career. And no idea what to do.

She squeezed her eyes shut. There was no one to blame but herself. She had booked this trip out of guilt. But instead of making her feel better, it had ruined everything.

With a deep breath, she snapped her eyes open. She had to fix this somehow.

Elle could call Travis's dad. But she doubted threats of taking away his trust fund would work this time. Travis didn't seem to care about earthly possessions right now.

He didn't have many close friends who could talk sense into him either. If she called Chris, the guy would probably just want to join Travis on his outdoor adventure.

Elle didn't want to wake up Sarah, if her yelling hadn't already done that. The pregnant woman needed rest, and Will was still recovering from his stomach bug.

Her head throbbed. This was all her fault. Why had she ever asked Mac to leave them alone?

Elle swallowed. Mac. Her last option. One she was desperate enough to seriously consider.

Doubt curled in her stomach. But even if she did convince Travis to come home, could they go back to the way things were? Sure, they were more like friends than a couple. But it had worked for them all this time. It was just fine.

She bit her lip, glancing at the ring on her nightstand. What was so wrong with fine? Fine was safe.

Elle took a deep breath. She had been the one to bring Travis to Alaska. And she would be the one to bring him back.

CHAPTER FOURTEEN

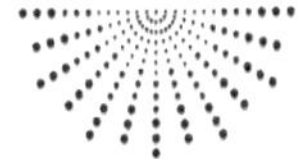

MAC

Mac's head pounded. Had he drunk that much last night? After he had gotten back from the lodge, it had taken him a while to settle down, and he had poured himself a sleep aid or two. But it had been far from enough to earn him a hangover.

He pried one eye open and then the other, praying he didn't see an empty whisky bottle next to his bed. No bottle. Then where the heck was the pounding coming from?

Mac squinted. It was louder now, metal rattling with each thud.

Goddammit.

He checked the time, scowling. He was an early riser, but it was barely on the other side of midnight.

Mac got out of bed, goose bumps rising on his arms in the brisk early morning air. He tugged on a sweatshirt and stomped over to the door. "Who the hell is there? Actually, never mind. I don't care. Just go away."

"It's Elle."

Even though her voice was muffled, it still sent a shiver down his back. He glanced at the warm bed.

Mac gritted his teeth. This wasn't the time to lose his head. Not only was the woman annoying as hell, but she still had a fiancé out in the forest somewhere. And, unfortunately for his hormones, Mac had morals.

He leaned closer to the door, raising his voice. "Go. Away. It's not even light out."

"It's almost morning."

As if that would make him open the door.

Tossing his hands in the air, Mac headed back to bed. She could knock until her knuckles bled for all he cared. He had earplugs, and Elle Blessing was bad news.

But then she said it. "Please."

The most pathetic, desperate *please* he had ever heard in his life.

Cursing under his breath, Mac stepped back and opened the door. Before he could even get one word out, Elle shot past him into the shop.

He blinked at her. How the hell had this woman made it into his house not once but twice? "Please tell me this is just a nightmare."

Elle twisted her hands, ignoring his sarcasm. "I need your help."

Mac took her in. Her hair was pulled up into a messy ponytail. Her big blue eyes weren't lined in black anymore. Her lips had lost their bubble-gum-pink color.

And dammit if she had never looked so good.

Mac took a deep breath, reminding himself that Elle wasn't single. Not to mention, she was the reason he had been up all night. That thought helped cool his jets. "What now?"

Her lip quivered, and before he could help it, Mac felt bad enough to care. He gestured for her to take a seat in his chair.

"Let me get you something to drink. I'm going to assume that you stole the truck again, so I'll keep it light. No need to top off this crazy night with drunk driving."

She stuck out her bottom lip. "I didn't steal it, okay? At least not this time." Elle glanced away. "Sarah was up when I left. She told me I could take it."

Mac grunted, filling a glass with water. "I don't like how chummy you're getting with my sister. We have enough sibling rivalries without you turning her against me."

Elle rolled her eyes. "You have nothing to worry about. I can't get away from this place fast enough."

He handed her the glass. "So, we'll find your lap dog, and you can get out. It won't hurt my feelings if you head home early."

She glared at him. "That's why I'm here. I found Travis. Or rather, he found me." Elle took a sip of water.

Mac frowned. "That's good news, right?" She didn't seem that happy about it.

She nodded, her blonde ponytail bobbing. "It would be. Except he doesn't want to go back."

Mac cocked his head. "What do you mean?"

Elle held his gaze. She had to be wearing contacts. No one had eyes the exact color of sapphires. "Exactly that. He doesn't want to go back. At all." She shook her head. "It's complete bullshit. Something about realizing his purpose or whatever. And nature."

Mac lifted an eyebrow. He hadn't heard Elle curse before, but he had quickly learned this was a woman who constantly surprised him.

"He said I could keep the ring." She let out a bitter laugh. "As if I was only in this for a giant diamond."

Mac rubbed the back of his neck. What was he supposed to say? He wasn't exactly a relationship expert. That required actually having had a relationship. But he knew a thing or two about dumbasses. "Maybe you're better off to leave him here. Let him learn the hard way. He'll run home with his tail between his legs once we get within throwing distance of winter."

Her pale brows knit together, so fine and fair they reminded him of winter frost on a window. "You don't get it. We have a life together. Not to mention my career. If I go back to LA without him, I'll lose everything."

He shrugged. Finally, a problem with an easy solution. "Then leave that shithole."

Her lips twitched, and Mac found himself thinking all kinds of things he shouldn't be.

Focus.

This was Elle. Engaged Elle. She-devil Elle. Elle who made his ass twitch. Not kissable, delicious, too-gorgeous-to-be-real Elle. "You've been to LA before?"

Mac shuddered. Now, there was a topic that would drive any thoughts of passion from his mind with all due haste. "Once. It's disgusting."

Elle studied him like a piece of art that she couldn't quite get the point of. "I wonder what the world is like to someone like you."

Mac frowned. What was that supposed to mean? "Someone like me?"

Her mouth curved up. "You can just be yourself. Nothing to hide. No secrets."

He shifted his feet. He didn't like the direction that this conversation was going in. It was a little too close to feelings for his taste. "Why are you here? You found Travis. You don't need my help anymore."

"That's where you're wrong." Elle set her jaw. "You're going to fix Travis. He will come home with me. And we will continue our lives in Los Angeles. Uninterrupted."

"You're nuts."

But the look on Elle's face was as serious as a heart attack. "You broke him. You fix him. This is your fault."

"My fault?" he scoffed.

She clenched her free hand. "If you hadn't left us alone in the woods yesterday, this wouldn't have happened!"

Mac ran his hand over his face. "Where do I even start? The part where you want to lie to everyone about you two being hunky-dory? And ask Travis to forget about his purpose or whatever bullshit? Or how about that you're the one who told me to leave you alone on the trail?"

Elle didn't flinch, her gaze unblinking. "It's not a lie. It's an arrangement that works. Something you wouldn't understand."

Mac didn't know if he should laugh or scream. But he knew that there was no way in hell he was going to be part of this ludicrous plan.

If the lap dog wanted to live on tree roots and bark, let him. Mac would pick that fate over the hellhole known as LA any day of the week. Damn place was a shanty town of broken dreams.

"I think it's time for you to go."

"Why?"

"Why?" he parroted. He began counting off on his fingers. "First, I had to fly your cute little butt out here. Next, I had to take you on a hike. Then I had to go looking for your fiancé in the middle of the night." He spread both hands wide, splaying all ten fingers. "Then I had to get up at this ungodly hour to entertain your wild plan."

Mac dropped his arms to his side. "Did it ever occur to you that I'm not on vacation island? I have a flight later today, and I need to get a certain amount of sleep so that all the passengers live, including myself. Got it?"

She stuck her chin out. "So you won't help me."

"Finally, we have an understanding." Mac took the glass

of water from her, setting it down. He placed his hand on her arm and walked her to the door. "Have a good day, sweetheart."

Mac closed the door behind her and waited, his shoulders sagging only once he heard the truck starting up and the crunch of gravel.

He tugged on his beard. Was he going soft? He had never let anyone walk all over him like this.

For a moment, he had even considered helping her. As if traipsing around in the woods at night wasn't bad enough. But she was the one who had come into *his* world. She could well enough find her way back on her own.

Mac poured himself his own glass of water and headed back to bed. Maybe he really did just need a good night's sleep for everything to make sense again.

The sheets had gone cold. He burrowed into the covers, reminding himself the bed was just big enough for one.

Mac did the math. Elle only had two more nights on the island. Two more nights, and then he would drop her off in Ketchikan and never look back.

He squeezed his eyes shut, but he still saw a blonde ponytail.

With a huff, Mac rolled over to face the wall. He sure hoped that his trip to Juneau would get rid of all these wacky thoughts.

No matter what, Mac had to stick to the plan to interact with Elle as little as possible. Because he had the feeling that the closer he got to her, the harder it would be to stay away.

CHAPTER FIFTEEN

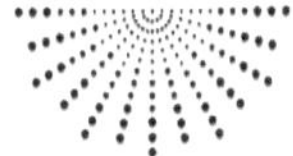

MAC

Fat drops of rain smacked against the windshield as Mac taxied his plane across the dark water to the dock. He gritted his teeth, feeling no better than when he left Darling yesterday.

How the hell had everything gone so wrong?

His plan had been to blow off some steam and come back with a clear head, but things had devolved. Starting with the fact that he had drunk too damn much.

When he craved female company, Mac made sure to get his kicks out of town. Even if there weren't approximately zero dating options in Darling, he didn't need to fuel the gossip mill while tanking his reputation at the same time.

Even then, he was careful. Mac didn't socialize often and tried not to hit the same town twice in a row if he could help it. He wasn't proud of his behavior, but he never interacted with women who weren't looking for the same thing. Mac might not be a relationship guy, but he wasn't an asshole either.

Not that it seemed to matter. Once a woman heard he lived in Darling, then she really wasn't interested in anything serious. Even by Alaskan standards, it was a step down. A step no woman had to take, not with the male-to-female ratio in Alaska being what it was. The odds were not in his favor, to say the least.

After he had settled into his hotel room in Juneau, he had wandered into a bar on the same block. The night had started with a beer and a shot. It hadn't taken long for a townie with huge chocolate-brown eyes and red hair to catch his eye. Juneau was bigger than Darling, but it was still a small town by most standards. The locals were looking for someone new too.

After a few more drinks, Mac and the redhead had made their way back to his room. Then it had happened. The single worst thing that could happen.

He had found himself unable to rise to the occasion.

That had never happened to him before, and it was completely his fault. Mac had drunk one beer too many. That was it. Not the pair of blue eyes and pert nose that never seemed to leave his mind in the past few days.

Instead of feeling better after his trip out of town, his frustration had reached new levels.

As he secured his plane, Mac reasoned with himself. At least he had been able to pick up the alternator for the van. Even better, he was taking Elle back to Ketchikan tomorrow. Soon, he'd be rid of her, and his life could get back to normal.

Mac headed up the dock, the wood creaking with each step. That little twinge of sadness he felt at the thought of never seeing Elle again? Probably just the hangover talking.

He felt sorry for her, sure. But she'd land on her feet. People got dumped every day of the week. Yet the Earth kept spinning.

What was Mac supposed to do anyway? Drag Travis out

of the forest by his ears and use puppet strings to make him say *I do?*

His shoulders relaxed as he walked up to his shop. The metal building wasn't many people's idea of a dream home. But this place was his, and behind those walls, he was unbotherable. After his disaster of a night in Juneau, Mac had never been happier to see the place he called home.

He opened the door, his jaw hitting the floor.

All the lights were on. A suitcase was propped up in one corner. And a cot had been pushed against the wall. Elle stood in the middle of it all, looking like the cat that ate the canary.

"What the hell?"

She blinked innocently. "Something wrong?"

Mac glared at her. He was not in the mood for this. "Breaking and entering comes to mind."

"I'll leave when you make things right with Travis." Elle crossed her arms.

Mac barked a laugh, deciding his promise to Sarah was officially null and void now that Elle had infiltrated his home. "You're actually crazy. I suspected it, but oh man. Now I know for sure."

She eyed him like a predator sizing up its prey. "What I am is not going anywhere."

Mac ran his hand over his face. It was a twisted joke, really, that a woman as gorgeous as Elle could be so completely infuriating. "You're just gonna squat here until I get the lap dog back in your lap? Is that it?"

She cocked an eyebrow. "You're smarter than you look."

Mac stomped over to her. He leaned in, instantly regretting it as her daisy scent made him light-headed. "Be careful what you ask for. I'll help you. But the vacation experience is over. No more Mister Nice Guy."

"That was you being nice?"

Mac's body turned hot. This woman could push his buttons like she had the cheat codes. "I'm going to call the shots. My island, my rules."

She smiled sweetly. "When do we get started?"

It was only then that Mac realized Elle had gotten exactly what she wanted. He clenched his jaw. Goddammit. "Tomorrow. It's going to be dark soon." His gaze wandered over her shoulder to the kitchen counters, cluttered with dishes. A large pot sat on the hot plate. "What is all that crap?"

She glanced over her shoulder. "Oh, that. Sarah loaned it to me."

With a growl, he whipped out his cell phone and tapped on his sister's name. "What the hell is going on?"

Sarah didn't miss a beat. "I take it you're home?"

His shoulders climbed to his ears. "And I take it you're an accomplice to this bullshit?"

Sarah let out a huff. "If the baby comes out spitting curse words, I know who I'm blaming."

Mac cracked his neck. He was pissed, but Sarah was pregnant. That took priority. He could at least rein in his temper for the length of a phone call. "You're changing the subject."

Sarah sighed. "It's not like I could help her look, and she wouldn't hear of Will being away from me for even a few hours. Loaning her a few things seemed like the least I could do after all that's happened. Some vacation this has turned out to be."

He glanced at Elle, then stepped outside. The fact that he had to leave his own home for privacy only further pissed him off. "It's time for her to go home."

"Have a heart, Mac," Sarah pleaded.

Mac shook his head. "You're just delaying the inevitable. Travis isn't lost, Sarah. He already found his way back once."

"Please. Just give her a few days. For me." Her voice grew

quiet. "I know what it's like when someone disappears on you."

He clenched his free hand. They barely talked about Sarah's ex-boyfriend these days. She was head over heels for Will and happier than Mac had ever seen her. But she had been through hell to get there. "Fine. A few days, that's it. But don't expect to get away with this crap once you aren't pregnant anymore."

"I wouldn't dream of it."

Mac could see the smug look on her face from his side of the phone.

They ended the call, and he went back inside.

Mac glanced at Elle as he stepped through the door. He couldn't deal with this right now. "I'm going to take a shower."

He grabbed a change of clothes and headed to the bathroom. Mac stepped under the hot spray, ready to wash the day off him. But after only a few minutes, the water sputtered and turned ice-cold.

Mac banged against the wall. "What the hell?"

The water switched back, suddenly scalding hot. He let out a cry as it burned his back.

Cursing under his breath, he toweled off and pulled on clean clothes. Damn woman was probably playing with the faucet just to piss him off.

Mac stomped around the corner, ready to give Elle a lesson on roommate etiquette.

His eyebrows climbed up his forehead when he saw the food plated on the table. And it wasn't from the Buck. He looked at Elle. "What did you do?"

"Witchcraft," she said primly. "What does it look like? Cooking calms me down, and we need to eat. If we can't go looking for Travis tonight, I might as well do something."

She opened a bottle of wine. As she pulled out the cork, Mac couldn't help but notice that her flashy ring was missing. Interesting. "I hope you like red."

He grimaced. "I'm not really a wine drinker."

The corner of her mouth turned up. "I figured."

Mac stared at her lips. She really did have a kissable mouth.

He blinked. Where the hell had that come from? Suddenly, a glass of wine seemed like a good idea. "But alcohol is alcohol, after all." He jerked his thumb at the table. "You didn't have to do all that, you know. I'm used to being on my own."

"I wanted to." Her shoulders slumped forward. "I wanted to do something normal."

Mac gulped his wine. He was already kicking himself for agreeing to this arrangement. He may have only promised Sarah that he'd help Elle for a few days, but Mac already knew that he'd do whatever it took to make things right.

And it didn't have a damn thing to do with Elle's sweet mouth or her home cooking. Those were just coincidences.

Mac sat at the table, reaching for his fork. His mouth watered at the sight of homemade spaghetti and meatballs.

"Try not to drool like an animal." Elle sat across from him. "Oh, and speaking of animals, I already fed the dog."

Mac paused with his fork in midair. "The what?"

She stared at him. "The dog. Your dog."

He frowned. "I don't have a dog."

Elle knit her brows together. "You sure? She seems pretty convinced she lives here. She's been hanging around all day. Friendly. Well-behaved." She paused. "On second thought, you're right. She might not be yours."

Elle stood and walked to the door. She opened it and whistled, and sure enough, a damn dog trotted inside. It was a husky, no doubt, with black-and-white fur and ice-blue eyes. "I assume you let her inside. You seem to be one with the animals."

It wasn't a compliment.

Mac gaped at the husky. "I have never seen this dog before in my life."

As if summoned, the critter came over and sat in front of Mac. He reached his hand out, and the dog gave it a lick.

"Then whose dog is it?" Elle asked. "As you've pointed out, this isn't Los Angeles. You've got to know who she belongs to, right?"

He shook his head. "I'm serious. I have never seen this girl before."

Elle rubbed the dog's ears. "Well, I love her."

Mac sighed. "Of course you do."

Elle looked up at him. "She doesn't have a name tag. What should we call her?"

"Please don't," Mac groaned. "No getting attached."

This situation was spiraling out of control. First the woman, now the dog. He was collecting strays faster than he could figure out what to do with them.

Elle placed her hands on her hips. "Is that your life motto?"

Mac didn't miss the sass in her tone. "Look, we're going to find Travis, and we're going to find this girl's home too. Easy."

Hopefully. His small Alaskan haven was feeling more like Grand Central Station with each passing day.

Mac turned to his plate and shoveled in a bite of pasta. His eyes nearly rolled back in his head at the rich flavor. "Holy shit."

"Is that what they say in Alaska instead of delicious?" Elle tilted her head. "I guess I'm not familiar with the local slang."

Mac reached for his wine. This was why he lived alone. It

was better for his blood pressure. "Why can't you just take the compliment? It's good."

She twirled a bite of pasta on her fork. "It should be. I had to start from scratch. You realize you have no food here, right?"

Mac tensed as his blood pressure took a second hit. He didn't need this china doll poking around in his cupboards. She hadn't told him anything new.

Except now she was aware of how pathetic he really was. If his place could talk, it would scream the words *single man*. Something else he had never been worried about because no one ever came here. Until Elle.

"Thank you, Mrs. Hubbard," he snarled. "Good to know you've been keeping busy."

Elle rolled her eyes. "Everyone has been nice. A lot nicer than you, anyway. Grace even gave me a bag of coffee for tomorrow. She said it's your favorite blend."

He sighed. Great. Now everyone knew that Elle was running roughshod over him. "So that's the kind of person you are."

Elle stabbed her fork into her pasta, meeting his eye. "What kind of person is that?"

He held her gaze. "The kind who can charm the stripes off a zebra."

She looked down at her plate, her voice quiet. "I do what I need to do to get by, just like everyone else."

Except that wasn't true. In just a few days, he had seen what this woman was capable of. Even now, Mac doubted he knew the depths of her.

When they had first met, he had thought Elle was a timid little bunny, prey that he couldn't be bothered with. Now he realized the truth. They were two predators circling each other.

Mac was beginning to think Elle was the superior species.

If he was a dog, he probably would've rolled over to show his belly a long time ago.

He scooped up another bite. "I'm still not sure how the hell you managed this."

"So that must be the Alaskan version of thank you." Elle shook her head. "I'm going to need a notebook to remember all this lingo."

"Thank you." He tried not to choke on the words. "It's just that this is the most cooking that this kitchen has ever seen."

Before Elle could answer, an unfamiliar ringtone filled the small space, and she jumped up from the table and scurried to her bag.

The dog let out a low whine before lying at Mac's feet, her cartoon eyes turned up.

Mac snuck a glance at Elle. Her back was turned to him as she talked on the phone.

He tossed a meatball to the dog, who snapped it up and licked her chops.

"Good girl, Dickinson," he whispered.

Dickinson was his favorite poet, not that Mac would admit to that, or that he liked poetry in the first place.

He groaned. Did he just name the damn dog? At this rate, Mac was going so soft that he would just be a lump of dough wearing a flannel shirt by the end of the week.

After a few minutes, Elle came back into the room. "Sorry about that. Work." She set a hand on her hip as she took in the table. "You waited for me to eat? Just as I thought."

Mac stuck his last meatball. "What is?"

She sat down. "Your bark is worse than your bite."

He let out a huff as he picked up his glass. "That's what you think."

"Oh, really?" She smirked. "So I just imagined you naming the dog right now?

"Son of a bitch," he mumbled into his wine.

Elle twirled pasta on her fork. "And don't think I'm giving you any of my meatballs. If you want to feed your dinner to the dog, that's your choice."

Mac guzzled the rest of his drink. That's it. Starting tomorrow morning, no more poetry. He would go throw axes or something.

Mister Nice Guy was leaving and never coming back.

CHAPTER SIXTEEN

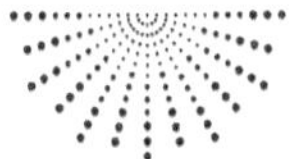

ELLE

It was hopeless.

They had been walking all morning. While the trail was flat for the most part, the forest was thick. The path wasn't always clear, and there would be times when Elle would have lost track of it altogether if Mac didn't part the tree branches for her to walk through.

Not to mention, the damn island was never not wet. That same constant mist chilled her to the core despite the fact that they hadn't stopped moving for hours. Darling must have a serious mold problem.

Her foot caught on something, and Elle tumbled towards the ground, reaching out her hands to break her fall. Before she hit the spongy forest floor, Elle jerked to a stop in midair, a strong arm tightly wrapped around her. Again.

As Mac helped her to her feet, her heart slammed into her ribs. Once again, he had saved her from getting hurt. Elle couldn't remember the last time someone had protected her like that, let alone twice. "Don't you know you're not supposed to do that?"

She glanced back at the offending tree root, hoping Mac wouldn't notice the color in her cheeks. She was embarrassed about tripping. It had nothing to do with the way her body warmed at his touch. "Fall? I'll work on it."

He snorted. "Reach out your hands like that. Good way to break an arm. Just hug yourself and tumble. Don't you know that?"

Elle looked up at him. "No one ever taught me how to fall."

"Then it's a good thing you keep me around."

She shivered. There it was again. That annoying flip-flop in her stomach.

He sighed. "Look, Elle. We've been out here for hours. You're cold. Your voice sounds as rough as mine. And we're making so much noise that I am pretty sure every bear on the island is paddling to Sitka by now. It's time to call it a day."

Elle swallowed. Mac had a point. As small as Darling felt, the actual island was big. Or at least a lot bigger than it seemed before she was searching for Travis. They couldn't cover the whole thing in one day, even if her feet weren't killing her.

The other problem was that she couldn't stay here forever. She had a career to get back to. The emails and texts from her manager were getting more impatient each day. The few photos she had posted weren't near enough. And the miniseries was hanging on by a thread.

Not to mention that Travis's dad had called twice, asking her to have Travis call him back because his son's phone kept going to voicemail. Elle had promised to pass the message along, skipping the part where Travis's phone was dead because the forest didn't have phone chargers. She had also left out that they were no longer engaged. Elle decided she'd let Travis explain that one himself.

Her head pounded as exhaustion and stress clawed at her. At some point, she had to call it and go back. And if she didn't find Travis, how the hell would she explain that?

None of which she would be dealing with if Travis hadn't run off in the first place.

She looked at Mac. "What do you think it is about this place?"

He shifted his backpack. "What do you mean?"

"Travis has everything. His family is richer than God. We have a huge condo with a view. He has me." Her voice cracked. "Why give all that up for this?"

Mac shrugged. "Probably because he was bored as hell. Never having to try? Having anything he wanted the minute he wanted it? Where's the adventure in that?"

Elle's shoulders slumped forward. "So I'm boring, then."

He chuckled. "Sweetheart, I haven't been bored since you got here. But that doesn't matter. This was never about you."

Elle kicked at the ground. "You're not making me feel better."

Mac blew air through his lips. "What I mean is that you can't blame any of this on yourself. The man has free will."

"I still don't understand. Why this place?"

Mac looked up at the canopy. "It's not so bad. Clean air. Nature. Peaceful."

Elle sniffed. "I suppose it is peaceful."

Although most of the time, the peace depended on Mac not being in the same room as her.

He cleared his throat. "Elle. Can I ask you a question?"

"I can't remember you once ever caring about my feelings, so please, go ahead."

Mac let out a deep breath. "What if Travis doesn't want to be found?"

"What do you mean?" Her heart sped up.

"He's not lost, Elle. He's choosing to stay away." Mac's green eyes rounded in sympathy. "It's not just that he found his way back before. When I went to the restaurant this morning to ask about the husky, someone mentioned seeing a new guy in town. Apparently, he bought some stuff at the store. His description sounded a lot like Travis."

Her throat tightened. "That can't be true."

Mac held her gaze. "Why not?"

"Because." Her voice cracked. "Because it means that I'm not enough."

That was it in a nutshell. No matter how big the diamond ring was or how many followers she had, there was always that fear in the back of her mind. That she was replaceable. That she really wasn't special at all.

Mac rested a hand on her shoulder, his touch gentle. "That's not what it means. This has everything to do with Travis and nothing to do with you."

Her eyes burned as her body grew hot. Elle would've paid money to not cry out here in the woods with Mac as her witness. But that didn't change the fact that it was happening.

She wiped at her nose, bracing herself for some smart-ass comment. But Mac stayed quiet, wrapping his arms around her and holding Elle close.

She shoved her face into his jacket as the sobs escaped.

What the hell had happened to her life? Travis had dumped her and disappeared. She was stuck in Alaska. Her career was falling apart. And the most annoying man in the world was the only one who seemed to give a damn.

She knew nothing at all.

Finally, her tears dried up. "Sorry," she mumbled into his jacket. Mac didn't actually smell as bad as she would have guessed. In fact, he smelled really good.

He patted her back. "Feel better?"

Elle stepped back with a sniff, looking up at him. "A little."

The corner of his mouth quirked up. "Good. Let's call it a day. The dog will be glad to see us, at least."

She nodded. "And we can keep looking tomorrow, right?"

"Tomorrow afternoon. I have a flight in the morning." Mac turned and started heading back up the trail, his long strides carrying him away quickly.

Elle plodded behind him when a crack in the forest startled her. She scurried to catch up. "Uh, Mac? Are there really bears out here?"

He turned to face her, flashing a teasing smile. "Don't you worry, sweetheart. There's nothing in the woods scarier than me."

Elle gulped. She'd never admit to Mac just how much she agreed. She had thought she knew who he was. A gruff, loner type who had no sympathy for anyone. But after today, Elle realized how vulnerable she was when it came to Maverick Carter. Nothing was more dangerous than that.

As Elle followed him back to the truck, she tried to organize her thoughts. She needed to find Travis and get back to Los Angeles. She needed to make sure her career didn't crash and burn. And she needed to keep a wall up between her and Mac.

Her shoulders sagged. Right now, those all seemed like impossible goals.

CHAPTER SEVENTEEN

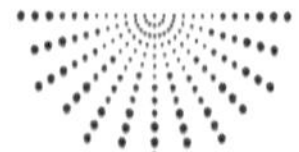

Elle had promised Travis that she would try not to work much during their trip. But that was before he declared his love for Mother Nature and disappeared into the forest. If he could break off their engagement, then she could check her damn email.

Once Mac had left for his flight, Elle had set up her laptop on the kitchen table, along with her travel light and camera. Maybe she could get some new content over to her team too.

She was halfway through her inbox when her manager called. "How are you not back yet?"

Elle's stomach twisted. If her manager was annoyed about Elle being one day late, how would she react to the news that Elle and Travis had broken up? But that wasn't a problem that had to be dealt with yet. Or at least not until they found him. "I'm sorry. We extended the trip a few more days."

Lacey breathed into the phone. "Are you serious? Look, I know you're having fun at the Blueberry Lodge—"

Elle's shoulders pinched together. It might not be a five-star luxury resort, but it wasn't that bad. "Salmonberry. It's called the Salmonberry Lodge."

"Whatever." Lacey let out a huff. "The cookbook is almost done. All your appearances have been scheduled. Everything is set to launch together. But if you aren't home in five days, there is no miniseries. They'll move on. It already took a miracle to get them to push back the meeting once."

Elle massaged her forehead with her free hand. "The cookbook is almost done? How? I've barely had a chance to work on it."

"Ghostwriter. You have more important things to do with your time than scribble recipes. We need your face out there, not stuck in an office for months."

Elle stood, her body hot. When had she lost track of what was happening in her own business? How was that even possible when she worked nonstop? "Lacey, I like writing the recipes. That's the foundation of my whole platform."

"Fine, whatever. I'm sorry," Lacey muttered. "I shouldn't have made that decision without you."

Elle paced the room. The husky watched her closely, following every movement with her ice-blue eyes.

She took a shaky breath, trying not to lose it. Elle was tired and stressed for reasons Lacey knew nothing about. This wasn't the time for personnel issues. Especially not when Elle was here and Lacey was handling almost everything in LA. She had hired Lacey because the woman was almost as hungry as she was. That was the point of her team. Not just to help Elle but to push her. "I'm sorry, I'm just a little surprised. But you're probably right. I have been really busy, and that's not going to change with the miniseries."

"If there is a miniseries." Lacey sighed. "Before you left, you were all about it. I thought if anything, you'd come back early, not late. What's going on?"

Elle's stomach knotted up. As much as she dreaded telling

people what had happened, Lacey should know. Sure, they had their tense moments, and Lacey might not know the exact details of Elle's relationship with Travis, but they had worked together for years. There was no one in LA that Elle was closer with—well, besides her former fiancé, of course. "Travis and I broke up."

Now to hope they found him later today so she didn't have to add the part where he disappeared and no one knew where he was.

"Is that all? God, you really had me worried for a minute. I thought you were going to tell me you were moving to Alaska for good or something." Lacey laughed. "We'll find a new Travis. That's easy. Now, get back here. Remember, you have five days."

The call ended, and Elle stared at the phone, her body numb. Not a single question about how she was doing? About Travis? No words of sympathy or encouragement? Only a solution so that the show could go on.

The husky whined, rubbing up against Elle's legs. She dug her hands into the dog's fur.

Her eyes burned as her chest grew tight. They could find a new Travis. The cookbook was already written. Elle's career had to keep going at all costs. How long would it be until she was the piece that they replaced? Would anyone even notice one cheerful blonde swapped out for another?

Elle sank down onto the bed, jumping up with a squeak when her thighs hit the rock-hard mattress.

She rubbed the back of her leg, frowning. She had been so distraught after the phone call that she had sat down on Mac's bed by mistake. Elle pressed on the quilt again. Something wasn't right. It was too hard to be a mattress unless Mac liked his bed as firm as his opinions.

A book, perhaps? Mac read every night. Except people

didn't keep books under the covers. Unless there was something to hide.

She chewed on her lip. Mac could be back any minute. Even if there wasn't a chance of getting caught, it was wrong to look.

But Elle was desperate for something to distract from the conversation with her manager and the feeling that her career could all come crashing down at any moment. It was either this or pour herself a glass of Mac's whisky. And she had never been much of a drinker.

With a glance at the door, she pulled the quilt back. Mac's juniper scent clung to the sheets, hypnotizing her and beckoning her closer.

A small leather-bound book lay on the bed. Elle reached for it and cracked it open. Neat, even handwriting that could only be Mac's lined the pages. Definitely not a novel. A journal, maybe? Or a log?

As she read the first page, her cheeks burned. It was neither of those things. It was a book of poetry. Poetry that Mac wrote.

Elle glanced at Dickinson. The dog's name made a lot more sense now.

Keeping one eye on the door, Elle flipped through the pages. Every word reached for her heart, squeezing it tight. So this was where he kept his feelings. Hidden.

Elle swallowed. Maybe she and Mac had more in common than she had originally thought.

She turned to the last entry, dated only a few days ago.

To be a different man
   To find love so easy
   Instead I have lost it
   Lost what I've never had

. . .

Sometimes wanting is enough
  But this isn't that time
  To know her love for me
  To complete design

Passion flames burn
  They warm, they hurt
  But I know this place
  Is cold without her

Her stomach sank. She was an idiot. Mac was completely and totally in love. And here she was, cramping his style. No wonder he seemed to have no patience with her. But Elle had been so focused on finding Travis that she had been oblivious to everything else around her.

Elle's hands shook as she closed the book, tucking it back beneath the quilt.

She had to make this right.

The logical place to start was getting the heck out of here and giving Mac his space back.

She jumped up from the bed, the husky trotting behind her. Elle was halfway to her laptop when the metal door slammed shut with a twang.

"What the hell is this crap?" Mac's voice boomed, bouncing off the metal walls.

Elle winced. He really needed to get some tapestries or something. The place was practically an echo chamber. But this wasn't the time for interior design suggestions. "Sorry. I didn't realize you'd be home so soon. I was about to clean it up."

"I see how it is around here." Mac scowled. "When the cat is away, the mouse plays."

She bristled. Was this really the same guy who wrote poetry? She wouldn't have believed it if she hadn't seen it with her own eyes. Elle reached for the light, packing it away. "I said I'm sorry."

"Do you not realize that?" Mac asked.

She glanced up at him. "Realize what?"

He scratched his beard. "I thought maybe it was just a coincidence. Every time you talk about work, you seem a little bummed out. But hey, most people don't like their jobs."

Elle slid her laptop into the carrying case. "What's your point?"

"My point is the minute you laid your hands on that stuff, you looked like your best friend just died. I've seen you smile, like when you caught me naming the damn dog. So I know you're capable of it." He gestured to the table. "But this sucks the happiness right out of you."

A rock settled in her stomach. This wasn't news to her. What was news was that it was so obvious to the people around her. "Like you said. It's my job. People don't work out of passion. They do it for money."

Mac peered at her. "Yeah, but you look like the before picture for an antidepressant. There's a difference."

Her vision blurred. Suddenly, getting out of here didn't seem like the best solution. It was the only solution. "I have good news for you. You won't have to look at my depressing face anymore."

He lifted an auburn brow. "Why's that?"

"Because I'm leaving. I'll go to the lodge. Or maybe back to LA." She shook her head, muttering, "Should've microchipped Travis."

Mac let out a chuckle. "Told you he's a lap dog." Elle glared at him, but Mac just held her gaze. That no-nonsense stare that made her squirm. No one looked at her like Mac. Sometimes she wondered if this man saw more of her in just a few days than others had her whole life. "So what made you decide to head out all of a sudden?"

"Because." Elle gestured towards his bed, flustered. "Because of the girl."

Mac scrunched his brows together. "Girl?"

"Woman, whatever. You're… I'm sorry." Her underarms prickled with sweat. "I didn't realize that you were in a romantic situation. I see now that being here was a mistake. Sorry."

He blinked at her. "Romantic situation? You're going to have to explain. I only have a country-bumpkin education."

Elle barked a laugh. Mac read classics, wrote beautiful poetry, and could fly a plane. If he was a country bumpkin, then she was a natural brunette and six feet tall. "Aren't you, you know, pursuing someone?"

"I fear not." He splayed his hand against his chest, his voice a falsetto. "Because this isn't eighteenth-century England."

"Jesus!" Elle stomped her foot. "You want me to say it? Fine, I'll say it! I found the book. The poetry. You're clearly interested in someone, whether or not she knows. And I am clearly the third wheel!"

Mac's face turned from pink to magenta to fire-engine red. "You read my poetry? My private thoughts? What the hell were you thinking!"

"I am sorry," she stammered. "I got a call about work, and I was distracted. I accidentally sat down on your bed instead of the cot."

"I told you your job was stupid." He ran his hand down his face. "I still don't get it. The book just jumped into your hands and opened up?"

"I am sorry. I am so, so sorry." Her chin quivered. "But the poems, they were beautiful. You have so much talent. It's sad you keep it hidden."

His fists clenched at his side. "I don't need to share everything I do with the world. I'm not like everyone else, sweetheart."

Elle nodded. After just six days of knowing him, she had learned that already. "I screwed up. I really am sorry. I'll pack up and see if Sarah can give me a ride back to the lodge."

Mac glanced at his watch. "Screw it."

He walked over to the kitchen cabinets, pulling out the bottle of whisky from the other night and pouring a glass. He held it out to her. "Care to join me?"

Elle twisted her hands. "It's early."

He shrugged. "Suit yourself."

She swallowed. Then again, after today, she could use a drink. "Fine. Just a splash."

Mac grabbed a second glass, tipping the bottle over it. He handed her the drink. "That's my girl."

She took a small sip, a tingle traveling down her back. It was from the burn of the whisky, not Mac calling her his girl. "I really am sorry. I know there is nothing I can say or do that'll excuse my behavior."

He studied her. "No one has ever done that before."

Elle shook her head. "I know what I did is awful. I am sure no one in town would—"

"No one has ever read my poems before." His voice was as quiet as the forest.

She shifted her feet. Elle had liked it better when he was yelling at her. She didn't know what to do with this version of Mac. "Why haven't you ever shared them?"

He sipped his drink. "Because they're stupid. Not to me, of course, but I'm guessing that's not how most people would feel."

Elle quirked up the corner of her mouth. "And you know

most people? I would be shocked if you even know some people."

Mac rolled his eyes. "Ha, ha. You really know how to make a guy feel better."

Guilt prodded at her stomach. Trust her to make a bad situation worse. Mac already didn't like her, and now he thought she was a snoop too. There definitely was no love lost between the two of them. "So, uh, do you want to talk about it? The woman in your poem?"

He threw back the rest of his glass, helping himself to a refill. "For some reason, I'm really not in the mood."

Elle cleared her throat. She could take a hint. "Okay, change of topic, then." She took another sip, the whisky scorching her throat and warming her up. But she wasn't looking for warmth. She was looking for courage. "Then how about I share something with you? I know it won't make up for what I did, but it's something."

Mac corked the bottle. "Let me guess. You're allergic to gluten."

"Okay, even if I were, that's a real allergy…" She took a deep breath. Courage. "The thing is, maybe you were right."

His jaw dropped. "Hand me my book of poems back. I have to write this down. The date you admitted I was right."

Elle smiled despite the tightness in her chest. She gestured to her work equipment on the table. "I'm not sure I like this anymore."

Her heart sped up. She had done a couple of brave things in her life. Elle had left home. She had started this career. She had agreed to get engaged, even though she had been terri-fied at the time. But this right now might top them all. She decided to tell the truth. "I'm not sure what I like at all, actually."

"Well, shit. Let's drink to that." He raised his full glass. "Need a refill?"

Elle held up her hand. "No, thanks. This is plenty for me. I normally don't drink at all."

"That's the problem right there." Mac tapped his temple. "Drinking rhymes with thinking for a reason. If you did, you might know yourself better."

Elle giggled, her shoulders relaxing slightly. "You know that's not true."

Mac sipped his drink. "I told you. I have a bumpkin education."

"Please," Elle scoffed. "You may be one of the smarter people I know."

"That so?" He sat down in his leather chair, leaning back as Dickinson curled up at his feet. "Then, my dear, you really need to meet some new people."

Elle swirled her glass. "On that note, I guess I should call Sarah and see about getting a ride back to the lodge."

Mac tilted his head. "Let's get something straight right now. There is no girl. If you want to leave, it's a free country. Just don't do it because of my nonexistent love life. It's not like you'll be here much longer anyway."

He was right. This wasn't real life. But the thought of taking thousands of photos a week, being glued to her phone, and resuming the facade of the cheerful blonde made her shoulders slump with exhaustion. Was it all worth it if she was replaceable at the end of the day? Elle had done everything right with her career, and still, it could all disappear in an instant. "Yeah, true. I have to go back eventually."

He lifted a shoulder. "Or don't. You just said you don't even know if you like it anymore. So why do it?"

"I used to like it. Cooking, I mean." Elle's throat grew thick. Now she was the one ready for a change of topic. She gestured to the shop, turning his question back on him. "How about you? Why do you do all this?"

Mac dipped his chin. "Easy. I know I like it. I wouldn't

want to be anywhere else. I love flying, and I love having my business. It's enough. There is no need to be a millionaire here. What would I spend it on, anyway? I want to be right here, on this island, forever. And that is why you'll never find love poems written by me."

He punctuated his statement with a slug of whisky.

Elle wrinkled her forehead. "I don't see what being happy has to do with being single."

"Don't you?" Mac rubbed the back of his neck. "What woman would want this kind of life? Or at the very least tolerate it? Being with someone isn't my destiny. I accepted that a long time ago."

Elle took another sip, her glass still mostly full. Maybe drinking did help thinking. At least Mac knew what he wanted, even if he seemed lonely. "I wish I knew my destiny."

It would make life so much easier. Something to guide her, to tell her if she should turn left or turn right. Then maybe she could be somewhere else, living a different life. She wouldn't be constantly under the magnifying glass, so afraid to want the wrong thing that she didn't want anything at all. Maybe then she could be happy.

"Your destiny." Mac snapped his fingers, jumping from the chair and startling the dog. "I know exactly how we can find Travis. Come on, let's go."

Elle blinked at him. "Right now?"

He pulled the truck keys from his pocket and tossed them in her direction. "You're driving."

Elle snatched them out of the air and set down her unfinished glass, following Mac out to the truck as the husky trotted behind them.

Her heart climbed into her throat. This was what she had wanted. Once they found Travis, they could go back to their lives in LA, albeit separately.

But what if she had it all wrong? What if real life wasn't the life for her? And why did none of that seem to bother her when she looked at Mac?

CHAPTER EIGHTEEN

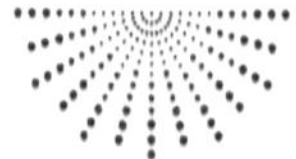

MAC

Mac called out directions while Elle drove. Maybe it was the whisky talking, but there was something satisfying about the way Elle handled his truck. She hadn't even hesitated when he had tossed her the keys.

He knew she could drive. It wasn't that. It was the fact that Elle was fearless. She had commandeered a vehicle, moved in on top of him, and kept going when anyone else would've given up. And though it got his hackles up that she had read his poems, there was also something exciting about sharing that part of him with her.

All that both intrigued and terrified him. Because the more he learned about Elle, the more he wanted to know. In fact, Mac was starting to think that he could never have enough of her.

But he couldn't expect an average woman to stick around Darling, and Elle was far from average. Even if she didn't like her work and was single, there were a million better options far away from here. Getting closer would be a mistake.

His gaze wandered to the side mirror, where Dickinson's head poked out over the truck bed, her ears pinned back as she faced the wind.

The corner of his mouth turned up. Damn dog was fearless too.

Mac rubbed the back of his neck, keeping a lookout for the turnoff. As much as he was enjoying the drive, he wasn't enjoying getting closer to their destination, even if it meant getting the answer they needed. He spotted the clearing and pointed. "Right there."

Elle took the turn, and they drove deeper into the forest. The truck bumped along the dirt road until a flashing white trailer stood out against the greens and browns of the trees. It was unnatural, like the woman inside.

Mac waved his hand. "You can park wherever."

It wasn't like this was a popular spot. People only came here when they were truly desperate. Like a woman trying to find her lost ex-fiancé. Or a man trying to protect his heart.

Elle turned off the ignition, looking around. "You think Travis is here?"

He could understand her doubt. There wasn't much to see. Besides the trailer, there was only a firepit and a couple of folding chairs. It looked like a life abandoned, or at least a life not cared about.

Mac swallowed. Is this how people saw him too? "Not exactly. We're here to talk to someone who might know where he is."

Elle adjusted the zipper on her jacket. "Why would this person know?"

"She's psychic." He shrugged. "Supposedly."

Elle arched a blonde brow. "You don't strike me as the spiritual type."

He snorted. "You can keep your crystal shops. But at this point, I'm willing to try anything."

"I see," she said quietly.

Mac told himself not to read into it. No good would come from asking questions. After all, they were here for answers.

Dickinson stayed put in the truck bed while they walked up to the front door. Mac took a deep breath and knocked, though she probably already knew they were there.

The door opened, and Natasha smiled up at them. Her fine blonde hair was mixed with gray, and a few lines fanned out from her bright blue eyes.

Mac shifted his feet. It was embarrassing to be scared of someone who looked so harmless.

"Maverick," she said in that lilting voice of hers. As far as Mac knew, Natasha had mostly grown up in Alaska. She had even been friends with his parents back in the day. But she still carried the slightest Russian accent.

Natasha focused her gaze on Elle. "You must be Elle."

Elle's eyes grew wide. "You really are psychic."

"Or it's just a very small town." Natasha winked. "Please, come in. I just made some tea."

The two women disappeared into the trailer, leaving Mac to follow.

He cracked his neck before stepping inside. Mac folded himself into a metal tube almost every day. No reason to feel claustrophobic in this tin can.

Three glass cups sat on the Formica table, steam rising. Elle turned to look at him, an eyebrow raised.

He shrugged. Yeah, it was creepy. But they were running out of options.

They joined Natasha at the table. She reached for the sugar bowl, adding a spoonful to her cup. "So you haven't found him yet."

Elle tilted her head. "You know why we're here? You know about Travis?"

"I do." Natasha stirred her tea. "But do you want to know where he is? Or do you want to know the truth?"

Elle frowned. "What's the difference?"

"Only you can tell me that." Natasha picked up her cup.

Elle glanced at Mac, and he lifted his hands. "If you want to know your destiny, here's your chance."

She looked back at Natasha. "The truth."

Natasha set down her cup. "The man in the forest is not the one who you'll marry. But you have already met the man you will marry."

Elle paled. "What does that mean?"

Natasha blinked at her. "I told you. The truth."

Elle jumped to her feet, bumping the table with her leg and sending tea sloshing from the cups. "I'll be outside."

The trailer door slammed shut behind her, and it took everything Mac had not to follow her. But they came here for answers, and he wasn't leaving without them. "Why the hell would you say something like that? No good can come from it."

Natasha stuck her chin out. "You aren't hearing me. Because it's the truth."

Mac smacked his palm on the table, the spoon clinking in the sugar bowl. "Just tell me where Travis is so we can find him, and they can go on their merry way home."

Natasha held his gaze. "That's what you want."

Mac gritted his teeth. "Is that a question?"

"Why did you come here, Maverick?"

He let out a huff. "You know why. We need answers. We've been looking for this bozo for days now."

"No. You came here to get answers to questions you didn't ask."

"Jesus Christ." Mac ran his hand down his face. "What the hell are you trying to say?"

She glanced at the door, then back at him. "You already

know what you want. I will not be the one to tell you that you can't have it. Life is too short."

Mac clenched his jaw. It was pointless trying to get a straight answer from Natasha. No wonder she didn't get many visitors. If she was lonely, it was her own fault. "Just tell me where to find this guy. Please."

"If that's what you want." She grabbed a pen and paper.

Mac's throat tightened as Natasha's hand moved back and forth across the page, a map coming into form. They could find Travis now. Elle could go home.

When Mac had imagined finding the guy, he had always thought of how relieved he'd be for his life to return to normal. Not how much he would dread it.

Natasha handed him the map.

"Thanks." Mac folded it and stuck it in his pocket. He pulled out his wallet. "What do I owe you?"

"Nothing." She smiled. "My only request is that you remember it's okay to have what you want."

He shoved his wallet back in his pocket and headed for the door. What the hell was a person supposed to say to that? "Uh, I'll keep that in mind."

Mac hightailed it to the truck before she could dispense any other nuggets of wisdom. He found Elle in the cab, sitting behind the steering wheel. Dickinson sat next to her in the middle seat.

He opened the passenger door. "I see the dog has been promoted to human."

"She was keeping me company." Elle scratched the husky's neck. "Sorry to run out of there. I needed a minute to myself."

He lifted a shoulder. "I get it."

Her eyebrows knit together. "And? Do you know where to find Travis?"

Mac pulled the piece of paper from his pocket, holding it up. "Yep. Got it right here."

"Then we can go get him," she said, her voice flat.

Elle didn't seem much more thrilled than he did.

Mac stepped into the cab. "We could. Or we could go tomorrow. What's one more day? I haven't even had a chance to show you around town yet." He rested a hand on his stomach. "You hungry? I'm hungry. Let's grab some dinner."

A smile played at Elle's lips, and she looked five years younger. "Were you ever planning on showing me around town? I thought you were counting down the days until I left."

He shrugged. "I was planning on showing you the bar."

Elle patted the dog's head. "What about Dickinson?"

Mac sighed. He really had gone soft. "We'll bring her."

This time, Elle did smile.

His heart skipped a beat. Making Elle smile was quickly becoming his new favorite thing in life.

CHAPTER NINETEEN

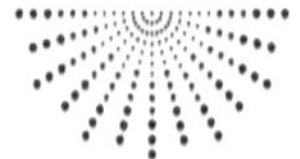

ELLE

What the hell was she doing?

Elle tightened her grip on the steering wheel. She should go get Travis right now. That was the only reason she was still here, right? Even if they weren't engaged anymore, it wasn't like she could just leave him in Alaska to fend for himself.

The man in the forest is not the one who you'll marry. But you have already met the man you will marry.

She shifted in her seat. It wasn't the first part of Natasha's prediction that bothered her. When Travis disappeared, Elle had genuinely believed that once she found him, they could go back to the way things were. But she had realized just how ridiculous that would be to ask of him. To ask of herself.

Elle swallowed. But what about the idea that she had already met the man she was going to marry? Only one person came to mind, and there was no way that could be who Natasha was talking about.

She glanced at Mac. He had been quiet since they had

started driving. Had Natasha said something to him after Elle had left? Or had he come to the same conclusion that she had? That the only possibility was impossible at the same time?

The forest fell back from the road as they came into town, the drive back seeming to take almost no time at all. That was one thing Darling had on LA. No traffic.

Elle pulled to a stop in front of the restaurant and turned off the truck.

Mac tore off his seat belt. "Oh, thank God. The bar."

Elle didn't move. Maybe this wasn't such a good idea. She was confused enough without adding alcohol to the equation. "If we're both going to drink, maybe I should go park at your shop. Then I can walk back and meet you here."

He gave her a look. "Why? We can pick up the truck tomorrow."

She twisted her hands. "You aren't worried about someone taking it if we leave it here overnight?"

"Spoken like a truck thief," Mac muttered. "If that was a problem here, do you think everyone would leave their cars unlocked with the keys in them?"

"What about the dog?" Elle pointed at Dickinson, scrambling for another excuse. "Are you sure she'll be okay? I could take her back to your place first."

Mac waved his hand. "Couldn't get rid of her if I tried."

She fiddled with the keys. "And don't you think it's weird that no one is missing a dog?"

"No weirder than the rest of this week. Which is why I need a drink. Let's go." He opened the door.

Mac stepped out of the truck and looked back at her. He jerked his thumb towards the restaurant, but Elle shook her head and stayed put.

He glanced up at the gray sky before walking around to the driver's side and opening the door. "What's wrong?"

Her throat tightened. She couldn't tell him the truth. That even though they had gone to Natasha for answers, Elle was more confused than before. "Nothing."

He bobbed his head in the direction of the restaurant. "Come on. Let's grab a beer, and you can tell me all about nothing."

Elle gave him a shaky smile. Dammit. How did he do that? Mac didn't just calm her down. He made her feel safe. "A drink does sound good."

His eyes crinkled. "A big one."

Elle nodded and stepped from the truck. Mac snapped his fingers, and the dog jumped out behind her. He tried to put Dickinson into a sit in front of the restaurant, but the dog just stared at him.

"I give up." Mac threw his hands in the air. "Clearly, I have a gift for attracting strong women."

Elle laughed as she followed him through the double doors of the Buckwild Bar and Grill.

The restaurant was nothing like she had expected, though that was true of her entire time in Darling so far. The large space was somehow still cozy and welcoming, and it smelled good enough to make her mouth water. An older woman stood behind the tap, looking more like someone's grandmother than a barkeep. Elle couldn't help but like the place.

They spotted two free spots at the bar and made their way over.

"Hi, Charlotte." Mac pulled out a barstool, taking a seat. "I promised this woman a beer."

Charlotte smiled at Elle as she tossed out a couple of coasters. "I'm guessing this woman is Elle? I've heard so much about you." Her gaze flicked briefly to Mac before landing back on Elle. "It's nice to finally meet you."

Mac's face turned pink. "Make it a big beer."

Elle bit back a laugh as she perched on the barstool next to Mac. "Nice to meet you as well."

Charlotte grabbed two pint glasses and pulled on the tap.

Mac scowled. "I said a big beer."

Charlotte shot him a look. "You know the rules."

"This is why I drink at home," Mac grumbled. "Fine. Chili, please."

Charlotte switched out one of the pint glasses for a large stein, glancing at Elle. "Did you want to take a look at the menu?"

"It's the only way to get a big beer," Mac explained. "They won't serve it on an empty stomach."

Elle nodded. She wasn't normally a beer drinker to begin with, but when in Alaska, she supposed. "I'm going to stick with the small beer, but I'd love to try the chili too."

"Coming right up." Charlotte winked at Mac before walking away. "Enjoy."

Elle glanced at him, but he seemed to be looking everywhere but at her. "You talked about me, huh?"

"More like complaining." He huffed, picking up his glass. "So what do you think of the beer? They brew it themselves."

Elle reached for her beer. She took a tentative sip, and her eyebrows shot up her forehead. Holy cow. It was amazing. The bitter taste was delicate and refreshing at the same time. "I can see why you wanted a big one."

He chuckled. "Keep drinking and you'll see why they make you eat before they serve it to you." Mac took a sip of his own drink, glancing back as a few more people walked in. "So what's bothering you? The phone call?"

Elle wrinkled her forehead. "Phone call?"

Mac rested his elbow on the bar. "Earlier, you said you had a call about work."

"Oh." Her shoulders slumped forward. That was another problem she had no idea what to do about. "Nothing. I mean, something. I have an offer for a TV show. Well, more like a miniseries, really."

"That's impressive. But I'm not surprised. Your stuff is pretty good."

Elle eyed him. "How do you know if my stuff is any good?"

"I looked you up, of course. Couldn't let a total stranger live with me."

She barked a laugh. "I'm surprised that you even have social media."

"I don't." He shuddered. "Just a normal internet search. I've never known someone with search results before."

An older man walked over, a bowl of chili in each hand. "So Charlotte wasn't joking."

Mac frowned. "Joking about what?"

The man set a bowl in front of each of them. "She said you were here with a woman. I had to see it for myself."

"Jesus Christ. I'm taking my beer to go from now on." Mac shoved his spoon into his bowl, and Elle rolled her lips in to keep from laughing. "Elle, meet Wolfie, Charlotte's lesser half."

Wolfie chuckled, stroking his mustache. "Couldn't have said it better myself."

The door to the Buck swung open, and another group of people walked in. As they made their way to the far end of the bar, one of them broke off and headed towards the jukebox.

Mac scowled. "We're going to need a second bar. It's getting crowded."

"Don't you dare," Wolfie scolded him. "I finally have paying customers."

As he went to greet the newcomers, the jukebox kicked on. Elle leaned in to whisper to Mac, trying to ignore the juniper scent that clung to his skin. On anyone else, it would be overwhelming. On Mac, it was perfect. "People don't pay?"

Mac sighed. "It's his own fault. People pay as they can. Sometimes more, sometimes less. He likes to tell us it all evens out, but who knows? I'm not sure how this place stays in business, but by some miracle, it does. I would spend a lot more time in Juneau without it. God knows they have more than one bar there."

"Well, I'm paying because this looks delicious." Elle spooned up some chili. The spicy dish was topped with shredded cheddar cheese and finely diced onion. "It's almost as good as the beer."

"I'm going to pretend you didn't just say that." Mac cringed. "Back to your problem. You don't want to be a big TV star or something?"

Elle set her spoon down, her appetite gone. There it was again. A reminder that this was all temporary. "The problem is that if I want to do it, I have to be back in five days."

He frowned. "Or what? You turn into a pumpkin?"

She reached for her beer, hoping that would get rid of the lump in her throat. "Or they'll find someone else."

Mac shoveled in a bite of chili, the melted cheese stretching between the bowl and his spoon. "That quickly, huh?"

Elle let out a dry laugh. "Trust me, there are a million blonde women waiting to do what I do. I'm replaceable."

Mac scooped up more chili. "So let them replace you and do something else. Seems like this whole thing is only stressing you out."

Her stomach twisted. He made it sound so simple. But he didn't know the truth. No one did. "I can't just walk away, Mac. It's everything."

"So?" He scraped his bowl. "You can make a new everything."

Her heart sped up, the idea as terrifying as it was tempting. But Elle had seen what her parents had gone through. Blowing up her life for something as fleeting as happiness wasn't just risky. It was stupid. "I wish it was that easy."

He pushed away his empty bowl. "Then I have a different suggestion." Mac turned on the barstool to face her, his leg brushing against hers and sending a tingle to her toes. "How about another round? If you're going to go back to all that not smiling and shit, it sounds like this is your last chance to let loose."

Elle shuddered. "One beer is already on the wild side for me. You know that."

"Might as well enjoy one day of your trip." He pointed at the bottles that lined the back of the bar. "What's your pleasure?"

Elle bit her lip. Mac was right. If she couldn't cut loose here, she couldn't cut loose anywhere. Didn't she deserve at least one day of fun after years of work? "It's been a while, but back in the day, tequila shots."

"A woman after my own heart." He winked. "If I had one."

Elle laughed and shook her head. The last few days, Mac had spent every spare minute he had between flights helping her look for Travis. He had taken in a stray dog. Hell, he had taken in a stray woman. He had a heart. Maybe the biggest heart of anyone she had ever known. "Fine. One shot."

Mac caught Wolfie's eye. "Two tequila shots, please."

The barkeep poured the amber liquor, passing the shot glasses across the bar.

Mac picked up both glasses and handed one to Elle. His hand brushed against hers, sending a jolt of electricity up her arm. "As long as we're cutting loose, there's one thing I want to get straight."

Elle held up her free hand. "Don't worry. Even if I had an

entire bottle of tequila, I wouldn't tell anyone about your poems."

"It's not about the poems. It's about you." He pinned her with his gaze, and Elle gulped. When was the last time someone looked at her like that? Had anyone ever looked at her like that? "The fact is you're not replaceable to me."

Elle sucked in a breath as her pulse quickened. For so long, she had been so afraid to make a mistake that she didn't even want anything because she was afraid it would be the wrong thing.

Until right now.

You have already met the man you will marry.

The jukebox and chatter and clinking glasses faded away. Elle could hear nothing but the beating of her own heart. This was it. She knew what she wanted. And just this once, she was going to let herself have it.

She leaned in, closing her eyes.

"Maverick," a woman purred. "I am so glad I found you."

Elle snapped her eyes open. A gorgeous redhead was looking at Mac like she wanted to eat him.

Suddenly, Elle was stone-cold sober.

CHAPTER TWENTY

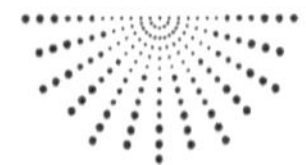

MAC

The redhead from Juneau.

Mac blinked. Had that only been a few days ago? Now, the idea of being with anyone but Elle was as appetizing as thumbtack soup.

He gulped, glancing her way. Elle didn't even look at him, but he could feel the anger rolling off her. He had to fix this. "Uh, Maddie. I'm actually here with someone."

Maddie pouted. "But I came all the way here to see you."

"You came here to see *me?*" Mac choked on the words.

"Yeah. My brother came out here to drop off an order, so I tagged along." She fluttered her lashes. "Thought if I ran into you, you could give me a ride in that plane of yours."

Mac's shoulders relaxed. Finally, an easy way out of this unwelcome interruption. "That's impossible. I've been drinking. Tequila." He threw back the shot, cringing as it scorched his throat. Hopefully that sent a clear message.

"You always did appreciate having a good time." She laughed, and the sound grated on him. Nothing like the tinkling wind chime of Elle's giggle. "We're sticking around another day or two so that my brother can do some hunting on the north end of the island. If you're free tomorrow, so am I."

Before Mac could tell Maddie he never planned on being free again if he could help it, Elle spoke up. "If you have the whole day, Mac does this really great thing where he brings a gourmet picnic and takes you out to a scenic spot."

Mac's jaw dropped. A picnic and a scenic spot? That sounded like some romantic shit. If he didn't know better, it seemed like Elle was trying to set him up. But that wasn't possible. Not when ten seconds ago, Mac would've bet his plane that she was going to kiss him.

Maddie's eyes lit up. "I would love that." She gave Elle an appraising look. "I'm sorry, who are you again? His assistant or something?"

Elle's smile turned brittle. "I'm no one. Just passing through."

Mac felt like he had been sucker punched in the stomach. No one? She was the only one.

Maddie pulled a pen from her purse and grabbed a cocktail napkin. "Here's my number. Let me know the details."

With a wink, she was gone.

Mac turned to Elle. "I can explain."

Elle slammed her full shot glass on the bar top. "No need. I need to get going anyway. I've got a picnic to make."

Mac tugged on his beard. Goddammit. A picnic she had suggested. "Elle, you don't need to do that, okay? I don't even want to do this flight tomorrow. And what about going to get Travis?"

She shrugged. "Travis will survive one more day. He knows how to find his way back. He was the one who wanted this. I would've been fine never coming to Alaska at all."

Elle stormed off, shoving open the double doors and walking out of the Buck.

Mac whipped out his wallet, fumbling as he pulled out a couple of bills to leave on the counter. After a moment's hesitation, he grabbed Elle's abandoned shot and threw that back too. Couldn't make things worse.

He scrambled to follow Elle, tripping over his own feet like an idiot. Jesus Christ. This woman literally had him chasing her. What parallel universe had he entered, and how the hell could he get back to normal life?

His stomach twisted. Normal life didn't have Elle. Suddenly, normal didn't seem so interesting.

The husky trotted behind Mac as he crossed the street to catch up with Elle. "Let me explain. I just met her last week, and—"

Elle whipped around, and Mac stumbled to a stop. "When did you meet her?"

Mac swallowed. His head was swimming from the beer and tequila back-to-back. Maybe that second shot had not been wise. "Uh, the day after Travis took off."

Her eyes widened. "Oh my God. The poem. That's who the poem was about. You lied to me!"

She spun on her heel and practically ran into Locke Grocery.

If it was physically possible, Mac would kick his own ass right now. Yes, he had lied about the poem. But even if he confessed to her who the poem was really about, it wasn't like she'd believe him now.

Mac told the husky to wait and followed Elle inside. She stood in front of the cold case, tapping her chin. "Do you prefer salami or turkey?" She opened the door. "Who cares? I'll make both. I am your assistant, after all."

He let out a gasp of exasperation. "Are you kidding me? You run the whole damn show!"

Elle placed the lunch meat in her basket and stomped over to the bread section.

Mac caught Vivian staring at them from behind the counter. He pressed his lips together. He didn't think Vivian was a gossip, but he wasn't about to take the risk. He wasn't in the habit of making good decisions lately, it seemed.

Mac stepped outside and waited with the husky. Elle made him crazy. That was the only explanation. He'd finally found a woman willing to set foot in Darling, one who didn't have an ex-fiancé skulking around in the woods, and Mac was chasing after one who would never choose this life. Never choose him. After all, an almost-kiss wasn't exactly a commitment.

It's okay to have what you want.

His throat tightened. If only who he wanted also wanted him.

Elle came out of the store, and they walked in silence together back to the shop. Even the husky was quiet for once.

When they were finally behind closed doors, Mac tried to explain again now that Elle had a minute to cool off. "Yes, I met Maddie after you got here. I was going crazy, okay? I couldn't stop thinking about you. Couldn't stop wanting you. It was the stupidest thing. You made me want to punch a hole in the wall and throw you up against it at the same time."

"Well then, it's a good thing you met Maddie. Because I'm going back to California. And this?" She gestured between the two of them. "Would be a horrible idea."

Mac set his hands on her shoulders. "Please, Elle. We're running out of time."

She looked up at him, her eyes glistening. "No. I'm just choosing not to waste mine anymore."

Mac's heart squeezed as she slipped from his grasp. Elle walked to the bathroom, slamming the door shut. The pipes shuddered as the shower came on. He ran a hand over his face. Perhaps the best thing to do right now was give Elle space. Everything he said only seemed to make it worse.

The husky came up to him and lay down with a whine. Mac leaned over to scratch the dog's ears. He wanted to lie down and cry too.

Instead, Mac put the groceries away and stepped outside. He walked to the dock and looked out at the water. His plane bobbed as dark waves lapped against the dock.

Mac sucked in a deep breath. This was everything he had. His whole life. For him, it was enough.

He had been upset that Elle hadn't let him explain. Confused that she had pushed him towards Maddie. But why should she put her heart on the line for something she didn't really want when she stood to lose so much more?

Maybe Elle didn't feel the same way about him that he felt about her. But he would still do anything he could do to make her happy. Unfortunately, it seemed that was a life without him in it.

CHAPTER TWENTY-ONE

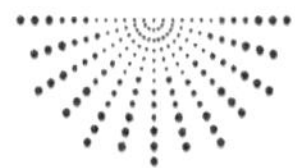

ELLE

"At least you didn't leave me for a redhead."

Dickinson whined, rubbing her face against Elle's thigh.

Despite her crummy mood, Elle couldn't help but smile. She'd never wanted a dog. She didn't have time for one. But after just a couple of days, Elle couldn't imagine life without the husky.

Her shoulders sagged. She would have to face that reality eventually, though. Even if no one claimed the dog, Elle was going back to California sooner or later. And after last night, she preferred sooner.

Her cheeks burned. She had sworn Mac was going to kiss her. Then Maddie had shown up, and Elle realized she'd had it all wrong.

Shaking it off, Elle turned back to her laptop. With Mac gone, she had planned to get some work done. Unfortunately, the only content she had been able to create was imagining what he was doing on his date. Especially now that he was late. Mac was never late.

Elle chewed her lip. She should've never suggested the picnic in the first place. But in that moment, all she could think about was getting space from Mac.

Her stomach knotted up. Why was she so bothered by the whole situation? She had done the right thing telling him to go. His last poem had to be about Maddie. It was written right after they'd met. Meanwhile, Travis was probably writing love poems to nature.

Elle rested her chin on her hand. It took a special kind of woman to get dumped twice in one week. Even if anything between her and Mac had only been in her imagination.

The husky whined again, nudging Elle's leg. With a sigh, she pushed herself up from the table and closed the laptop. Sitting here and driving herself crazy wasn't doing any good. "Come on, Dickinson. Let's go for a walk."

The husky didn't need to be asked twice, shooting over to the door and wagging her tail.

Elle slipped on her rain jacket and stepped outside. Whatever Mac was up to on his date, he'd be back today. And tomorrow, they would go get Travis. Then she would go home, and there would be nothing to do but work. Might as well enjoy one last walk with the dog.

But you have met the man you will marry.

She closed the door behind her and shoved her hands in her pockets, heading towards the water. For a brief moment of insanity, Elle had truly wondered if Mac was that man. Now, she realized how delusional she had been. It was a good thing Elle had her career because relationships were clearly not her strong suit. Maybe she'd tell her manager that she wanted to stay single for a while, even though Lacey was probably already holding casting calls for Elle's new boyfriend.

A shiver ran down her back at the reminder that everything could be gone overnight. Everything she had worked for, every right decision she had made, could be swept away with one bad one. Elle had to stay focused, and that included not obsessing about a certain grumpy pilot.

They walked along the water, the husky panting as Elle's boots crunched the gravel. When she had first arrived in Alaska, the silence had made her uncomfortable. Now, she craved it. For the first time in years, she could hear her own thoughts instead of constantly being told what to think.

They looped around and were almost back to the shop when Dickinson let out a whine and sprinted in the direction of Mac's dock.

Elle cocked her head, the drone of an airplane quickly becoming loud enough for human ears.

Her stomach twisted. The only thing worse than imagining how Mac's date went would be seeing him and Maddie together. But Elle didn't want to abandon Dickinson.

Dragging her feet, she joined the husky at the water's edge. Elle shaded her eyes against the glare of the cloudy sky, the plane growing larger with each passing minute. Dickinson sat next to her, studying the sky just as intently.

Elle quirked up the corner of her mouth. She could only imagine what Mac must think about his newfound roommates waiting for him. Probably something along the lines of a four-letter word.

As he brought the plane in for a landing, her body prickled with sweat. Another reason she and Mac would never work. A nervous flier and a pilot? She couldn't imagine a worse match.

Elle forced herself to take deep breaths. This was Mac. He knew what he was doing. There was nothing to worry about.

But just as the plane touched down on the water, it flipped over, crashing top-first into the sea.

A scream clawed at her throat. This wasn't happening. Not to Mac.

It seemed like a lifetime ago that Mac had given her the preflight safety speech back in Ketchikan. That the plane could catch an edge on landing and what to do if it did.

Elle had thought nothing could be worse than living through her biggest fear, but she had been wrong. It was so much worse seeing it happen to someone she cared about.

Her heart pounded. Time seemed to slow down as the plane bobbed, the legs sticking up in the air like an overturned bug.

Elle felt like she couldn't breathe.

One second.

Two seconds.

Three seconds.

No sign of Mac.

She tore off her jacket and tugged off her boots. Elle ran to the end of the dock and jumped in the water, the frigid sea knocking the breath out of her.

It wasn't her first time in cold water. She had gone ice swimming as a kid. But then, there had been a ladder. There had been help. All she had now was fear.

Elle pulled herself through the rolling sea as it pushed back against her. No matter how hard she swam, it felt like she never got any closer to the plane.

Finally, a head emerged, auburn hair dark and slicked down.

"Mac!" Elle tried to scream, but her voice didn't sound louder than a whisper to her own ears. "Mac!"

He turned to face her, and his eyes grew wide. "Son of a bitch. You brought the damn dog?"

Elle twisted to see Dickinson paddling behind her. She hadn't even heard the husky jump in.

Mac grabbed Elle's hand, pulling them to shore. He didn't

seem to be struggling half as much as she was. "We need to get out of the water before your ears turn blue and fall off."

Elle looked over her shoulder, trying not to lose her grip on Mac's hand. "What about Maddie?" She might not be a big fan of Mac's date, but she wasn't about to let the woman drown.

Mac spat out a mouthful of seawater. "She's not here. Let's get on dry ground, and then we can talk."

The husky paddled ahead of them. Mac stayed with Elle, his big hand gripping hers tightly. If she had a single breath to spare, she might have told him thank you.

As she slapped her hand onto the dock, a wave of relief passed over her. Even without her jacket and shoes, her clothes had grown heavy. She felt light-headed from struggling to breathe as she swam through the freezing water. Her limbs were numb and clumsy. Mac may have been the reason she jumped into the sea, but without him, she might not have made it back out.

He climbed out of the water first before reaching for Elle. She shivered as she stepped onto the dock. They hadn't even been out of the sea for five seconds when the husky shook, drenching them again.

Elle shrieked, and Mac let out a raspy chuckle. "Damn dog."

He wrapped one hand around Elle's back and the other behind her knees, swooping her up without so much as a grunt. "Let's get you inside."

Elle's teeth chattered so hard that she couldn't even tell him to put her down. Not that he would've listened anyway.

Once they were in the shop, Mac set Elle gently to her feet in front of the bathroom door. "You shower first. You have hardly any body fat to begin with, and you need to warm up."

She swallowed. Based on the firmness of his chest, Mac didn't have much body fat either.

Mac grabbed her pajamas from her suitcase, setting them in her hand and ushering her into the bathroom.

As soon as he closed the door behind her, Elle moved as fast as she could, or tried to. She fumbled, her numb arms slowing her down. The scalding spray felt like a thousand needle pricks on her cold body, both painful and delicious at the same time.

Elle scrubbed the salt from her skin while trying not to use up all the hot water. She had learned that the hard way. After she tugged on her pajamas, Elle stepped out of the tiny bathroom. "Your turn."

Mac stepped inside with his own change of clothes and shut the door behind him.

Elle pulled a sweater over her head before working the towel through her hair. She hadn't even wanted to take the time to dry it. Not while Mac was out here, soaking wet and freezing.

In California, she wouldn't have set foot outside without her hair and makeup done. But here, that all seemed so pointless. The minute she stepped outside, the mist clung to her anyway, turning her silky-smooth hair into wild waves. Then again, so much that used to be important now seemed pointless.

Dickinson came up and gave Elle a sniff. The dog was always curious about the smell of Elle's shampoo.

She touched the dog's fur. It was still damp but not soaking wet.

Elle smiled to herself. Mac must have toweled her off. Did he always put everyone else first?

She cranked up the space heater. Despite the hot shower, Elle was still chilled to her bones, a mix of freezing water and the panic of seeing Mac crash.

Elle closed her eyes for a moment. Everything had happened so fast. Everything had happened so slow.

The pipes shuddered as the water turned off. A few minutes later, Mac came out of the bathroom, his face red from the hot shower.

Elle's chest heaved, once again relieved at the sight of him. Not even an hour before, she had been terrified that she'd never see Maverick Carter alive again. But all those feelings, everything she really wanted to say, got stuck in her throat. "Your plane?"

Mac took a step towards her. "Luckily, my phone still works. I called some guys while you were in the shower. They're coming over to help me flip it right now."

Elle nodded. Hopefully, it would be okay. If not, hell, she'd buy him a new plane. That was replaceable. She couldn't buy a new Mac. "And Maddie? Where is she?"

Mac moved another step closer. "Ah, well, I don't think she and I will be spending much time together."

Elle perked up, suddenly feeling much better than she should have after taking a dip in the Alaskan sea. "What happened?"

"Somehow, she got the idea in her head that this picnic was a date." Mac shook his head. "I let her know I felt differently, and about the time she poured her glass of iced tea over my head and tossed the sandwiches into the water, I figured the picnic was over."

Elle gasped. "She threw my sandwiches in the water?"

"Your sandwiches." Mac smiled. "Don't worry. I fished them out, though I think it's safe to say they're ruined at this point."

Elle bit the inside of her cheek to keep from giggling. "And then?"

He sighed. "And then I took her straight back to Juneau."

The knot in Elle's stomach came undone. "That's why it took you longer to get back."

Mac shrugged. "Figured I had already pissed her off real good. Least I could do was accommodate that special request."

Elle smiled. Mac might be rough around the edges, but he was a true gentleman beneath all that flannel. "That was nice of you."

Mac's lips twitched. "Let's just hope she returns the favor and she doesn't have her brother cut off our supply chain."

Elle tilted her head. "What does he supply the town with?"

"Toilet paper."

Elle laughed, her shoulders relaxing as feeling came back into her fingers and toes. "Well, I'm glad you're okay."

Mac shuddered. "Minus the emotional damage. That's why I don't mess with redheads. Not my type."

Elle cleared her throat, her pulse quickening. "Oh yeah? What's your type?"

"Always been partial to blondes." His gaze settled on her head.

She glanced at the heater. Suddenly, the room seemed too hot. "Oh?"

Mac took a few steps towards her, so close that she could see freckles dotted across his nose. "You were worried about me."

Elle swallowed. It wasn't a question. "I was worried about you *and* Maddie."

Mac lifted an eyebrow. "Interesting. Because you practically pushed me out the door with her."

Her cheeks were on fire. "I did. It was silly. It—"

But she didn't get to finish. Didn't get to tell him all the logical reasons she shouldn't care.

In an instant, there was no space left between them. Mac was right in front of her.

His hands cradled her face, looking down at her like she was everything that mattered. Like she was the only thing that mattered.

He kept an inch between them, asking her a question without saying anything at all.

Elle nodded. Something about his green eyes and his juniper scent and the fact that he was warm and she was cold made her say yes.

Mac lowered his mouth to hers, his kiss driving the chill from every square inch of her body.

She pushed into him as a moment of clarity came over her. If this was the only kiss she ever shared with Mac, she would remember it forever. This singular moment was what all others would be measured against.

Elle melted, intertwining her fingers in his damp hair. She wanted more. She wanted everything he was willing to give her.

A ring blared out, and Elle jerked away.

Mac cursed, pulling his phone out of his pocket. He shot her an apologetic look. "I have to take this. It's one of the guys helping me with the plane."

He tapped on the screen, stepping away as he took the call.

Elle pressed the back of her hand to her forehead. What had she been thinking? She was probably desperate after going so long without any intimacy.

But she was going back to California. And Mac was staying here. Why start something if she already knew it would end?

Mac walked back over to her. "I'm so sorry, but the guys are on their way over now. I better go meet them. The less time the plane is in the water, the better."

Elle waved her arm. "Yeah, of course. Go."

Mac opened his mouth, as if he wanted to say more. But

he pressed his lips together, leaving her and Dickinson alone in the shop.

Elle reached up to touch her lips, still tingling.

Suddenly, she saw everything so clearly. How easily she could fall for this guy. And how stupid that would be.

CHAPTER TWENTY-TWO

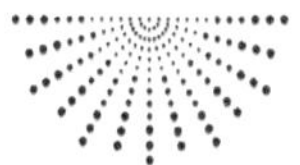

ELLE

Elle yawned and poured herself another cup of coffee, even though it was closer to lunchtime than breakfast. She had barely slept all night. Elle doubted Mac had gotten much sleep either. She had listened for his soft snoring, but it never came.

He walked over to her, and her pulse quickened. They hadn't talked about the kiss. After he left, Mac had spent the rest of the day working on his plane. Should she say something? Would he? Mac brushed past her.

"Any coffee left?"

Her shoulders drooped. Apparently not. But it was for the best. Elle would be gone soon, and eight days wasn't enough time for feelings anyway. Mac must have come to the same conclusion. She stepped aside. "Yes, plenty."

Mac grabbed the coffeepot, refilling his mug. "I got something to run by you. Sarah invited us to brunch. We're supposed to be there in a couple of hours."

"Brunch?"

Mac rolled his eyes. "Brunch. Have you heard of it?"

She glared at him. Apparently, he had gone back to being the same curmudgeon she had first met. On the bright side, that would make it all the easier to say goodbye and never look back. "I live in LA. I know damn well what brunch is. It's just that we're supposed to go get Travis today."

He shrugged. "I mentioned that to Sarah, and that's why she invited us over. She figured it was her last chance to do something nice for your trip." Mac slurped his coffee. "We'll swing by the lodge for a bit, and then we'll go get Travis after."

Elle raised a hand to her right eye. It was doing that thing, that twitch it did when she felt pushed over the edge. Although she had no idea why it was happening now. Just because it might be one of her last days in Darling wasn't a reason to get worked up. Everything was perfectly fine.

Mac peered at her. "What the hell is wrong with your eye? You short-circuiting?"

Elle's shoulders pinched together. She had found the trigger. He was standing right in front of her. "Yes!"

"Jesus!" He threw his free hand in the air. "If you can deal with a plane crash, surely you can handle brunch with my family!"

Elle stomped out of the room. She had to get away from him before she totally lost it. Mac knew exactly which button to push and when. If she turned around, Elle would bet money he'd be wearing that smug look of his. Never mind pretending the kiss never happened. She'd prefer to forget it altogether.

She grabbed a few things from her suitcase and locked herself in the bathroom. Elle needed to get ready, but more importantly, she needed a break from Mac. She took her sweet time doing her hair and makeup.

Mac eyed her as they climbed into the truck, the husky panting between them. "You look different."

She shot him a look. "Is that your version of a compliment?"

Mac started up the truck. "Nope. My version of an observation."

She tugged on her seat belt a little harder than necessary. For being a poet, he sure had a way with words. "I did my hair and makeup. "

Mac grunted as they pulled away from the shop.

Elle gritted her teeth. "If you have something to say, just say it."

"I think you look better the other way. Nothing extra. Just yourself."

Elle's breath hitched. Mac had done it again. He had taken the anger from her heart and handed her back something that felt good. It wasn't fair that she could hate him and love him at the same time.

She gulped. Love? No. Love was off the table. Lust, maybe. But not love.

They drove in silence, the only sound in the cab the slap of the windshield wipers and Dickinson panting.

When they reached the lodge, Elle shot out of the truck, the husky at her heels. She needed to be around anyone other than Mac. All that together time was doing strange things to her head.

Elle opened the door, and Bart ran up to greet her, his scruffy little body wiggling with each wag of his skinny tail. She reached down to scratch his ears. "We have a friend for you."

The husky poked her head out from behind Elle, touching noses with Bart.

The two dogs sniffed each other cautiously before taking off towards the living room at a playful run, making Elle laugh. If only it could be so easy with people. The dogs seemed to get along better than she and Mac.

Elle made her way to the kitchen, where Sarah stood at the stove, stirring a pot. Or at least attempting to stir a pot. The woman's belly stuck out, forcing her to stand sideways to reach the burner. Elle squeezed Sarah's shoulders. "Something smells good."

"Nothing like you could make, but I'm doing my best. Homemade hot chocolate." Sarah smiled. "I'm so glad that I get to see you one more time before you go back."

Elle nodded, the ticking clock louder than ever. Soon, Darling would only be a memory. Another reason of a hundred reasons to keep space between her and Mac. "Thanks for inviting us. But I would've been happy to visit over a bowl of cereal. You didn't have to go to all this trouble."

"All the credit goes to Will. I couldn't have done it without him. I listed off my pregnancy cravings, and he made them happen." Sarah turned off the stove, glancing over her shoulder. "Where is my brother?"

Mac walked into the room, giving Sarah a kiss on the cheek. "I'm right here."

She narrowed her eyes. "You're being uncharacteristically sweet."

"That's my future niece or nephew right there. Gotta make sure you like me enough to let me spend time with them."

Sarah barked a laugh. "Sure it wasn't your near-death experience? Maybe reevaluating your life priorities?"

He tugged his mouth down. "So you heard about that."

"As if I wouldn't. You know how things are in Darling." She patted his arm. "I'm glad you're okay. Someone has to make sure this kid doesn't turn out to be a city slicker."

Mac cracked a smile. "Damn straight."

Sarah reached for the carafe for the hot chocolate, and like a superhero, Will raced into the room, grabbing it for her. "How did you know I needed help?"

He poured the hot chocolate into the carafe. "Sensed it. Laundry is done, by the way."

Will flashed a smile at Mac and Elle as he carried the carafe to the table.

A twinge of jealousy flared in Elle's heart. Even though she was used to doing everything by herself, part of her wished she had someone she could count on completely. She glanced at Mac, but he just looked bored. If nothing else, she could count on Mac to remind her why nothing should ever happen between them.

Sarah plodded behind Will, gesturing for Mac and Elle to follow. "I hope you're hungry."

The four of them gathered around the table, heavy with quiche, blueberry muffins, freshly brewed coffee, fruit salad, and the homemade hot chocolate.

Elle's mouth watered just looking at the spread. At least Mac's grumpy mood hadn't ruined her appetite. She helped herself to a slice of quiche, taking a bite. "This is fantastic. I think it might be the best smoked salmon I ever had."

Sarah plucked a muffin from the serving platter. "I have to give some credit to Mac and my dad. They do a batch of smoked salmon every year."

Elle glanced up to see Mac giving her that smug look. It's a good thing he lived in Alaska. His ego would be a tight fit anywhere else. "My compliments to your dad too."

Sarah broke off a piece of her muffin, popping it into her mouth. "I'll tell him when they get back from Italy."

Elle took another bite, enjoying the quiche a little less now that she knew Mac had contributed to it. "Have you heard from them? Are they having fun?"

"I've talked to Mom." Sarah glanced at her husband. "But Dad only seems to want to talk to Will."

"What?" Will lifted his hands in the air. "We both like history."

Elle's throat tightened, and she reached for the hot chocolate. Will seemed to fit seamlessly into the Carter family, from what Elle had seen. Meanwhile, she didn't even have her own family to fit into.

Will passed the fruit salad to Mac. "I'm glad to see the dogs get along. That'll make things easier when you watch Bart."

Elle stuck another bite of quiche. "Are you and Sarah going somewhere?

Will and Sarah exchanged a look before Sarah turned back to Elle. "Just Juneau for a couple of days."

Elle sipped her hot chocolate. "What's in Juneau?"

Sarah poured her own hot chocolate, adding a dollop of whipped cream. "Nothing."

Elle squinted, glancing around the table. Will and Mac were suddenly very interested in their breakfast too. "What's going on?"

Mac let out a sigh so loud it could be heard in California. "Jesus Christ. Just tell her."

Sarah set her cup down. "The hospital is in Juneau. For the baby."

Elle's stomach sank. Once again, she had been so wrapped up in her own life that she hadn't noticed what was right in front of her. "You didn't plan on me still being here by now."

"I didn't want to say anything." Sarah dropped her gaze to her plate. "You're dealing with enough right now."

Elle's face heated. If Travis hadn't already broken up with her, she would do the honors. He had put her in this position in the first place. Guilt curled in her stomach. But she had made the decision to stay on her own, forcing her way into these people's lives. It was time to go back. "When are you due exactly?"

Sarah tugged at the hem of her shirt. "Next week."

Elle set her fork down. "Then I need to find Travis and get out of here." She turned to Mac. "If we find him today, can you fly us to Ketchikan tomorrow? I'm sure my manager can set up the plane tickets for the rest of the way home."

Mac held her gaze, and for half a second, Elle wondered if he might ask her to stay. "As soon as you're ready."

She swallowed, but the lump in her throat refused to move. Even if he had asked her to stay longer, she would've said no. Right? They both knew this had to end eventually. Hell, it hadn't even begun.

Elle pushed herself up from the table, her eye twitching again. Unfortunately, her body didn't seem to get the logic. "I'm sorry, I need a minute. I seem to have something in my eye."

She turned to walk from the room. A chair toppled behind her, followed by heavy footsteps.

"Elle," Mac called out.

Before she could answer, a shriek came from Sarah, cutting straight through Elle's heart.

Elle spun on her heel, her underarms prickling with sweat. "What was that?"

"I think the baby is coming." Sarah's face was contorted in pain.

Elle's stomach dropped. "Now? Here?"

Sarah nodded, taking slow, deliberate breaths.

Will jumped to his feet, guiding his wife from the table to the sitting room. They walked slowly as Sarah braced herself against the wall with one hand while keeping the other on her back. The dogs wove around their legs until Will commanded them to stay on the dog bed.

Mac cursed, following behind Will and Sarah.

Elle twisted her hands as she took small steps into the sitting room. This wasn't happening. People didn't just give birth at brunch. "Maybe it's just false labor."

"Probably not." Sarah's voice was strained. "I've been having contractions on and off since this morning."

"Then why the hell did you invite us to brunch?" Mac yelled, drawing a howl from the husky.

Will helped Sarah to the couch. "We need to make space."

Mac shoved the coffee table to the side, opening up the middle of the room.

Elle took a shaky breath. She couldn't just stand here. "What can I do?"

Will pointed over her shoulder. "We have totes in the office with everything we need. Can you go get them?"

Elle hurried to the office. She spotted the totes, stacked against the wall. She grabbed at the top one, but it was too high.

Standing on her tiptoes, Elle reached for it again. A big hand covered hers, and the tote lifted. Elle turned, and Mac arched over her, only a few inches between them. She stuck her chin out, mentally reciting every reason why getting closer would be a mistake. Needing every single one not to care that she could feel the heat radiating from his stupid muscled body. "I don't need your help."

His eyes crinkled. "Kind of reminds me of the airport when you wanted to carry your own bags."

Elle stared at him. He remembered that? Sarah screamed again, bringing Elle back to the moment. *Focus.* "Fine. I guess you can help this one time. I'll get the next one."

With a sarcastic bow, Mac carried off the tote. Elle stuck her tongue out behind his back, a new reason to stay away from him in her arsenal.

Once they were back in the living room, Will went

through the totes, setting up everything he needed. Meanwhile, Mac and Elle managed to work together to spread out clean linens and create a makeshift bed for Sarah.

Soon, Sarah was on the floor, propped up with pillows. Will stood at her feet, his hands thoroughly scrubbed and pink. He smiled at her. "We can do this, honey. We're ready."

Sarah nodded, looking slightly less serene as sweat dripped down her face.

Elle gulped. They were prepared for a home birth. Why shouldn't they be? Of course the island didn't have a hospital. It didn't even have fast food.

She winced at the sight of Sarah on the floor writhing in pain. No, this wasn't the life for Elle. Travis could come back or not. Elle wasn't staying here. She wanted medical care, comforts, and convenience.

Elle took a deep breath. She wasn't the one who needed help right now.

With Will at Sarah's legs, there was no one by her side. Elle lowered herself to the ground, holding Sarah's hand and smoothing the hair away from her face.

Mac paced the room, his signature swagger gone. The more in pain Sarah was, the more terrified he seemed.

But Sarah was oblivious to her older brother as she huffed and puffed her way through the birth, a vise grip on Elle's hand. Sarah and Will were in their own world as he coached Sarah between screams.

After what felt like forever, Will finally yelled out. "I see the baby!"

Excitement welled up in Elle's chest, and a smile appeared on Sarah's blotchy face. Mac, however, looked a shade paler.

Will rubbed his wife's legs, murmuring words of encouragement. "You can do this, honey. Keep pushing."

A short while later, a fifth voice cried out in the room.

Sarah let out a sob, flopping back on the pillows while Will took immediate care of the baby.

Elle shook as she sat back. Holy shit. They had done it. She looked down at her hand, wiggling her fingers. Not broken.

She glanced up to see the dogs watching the scene closely from the dog bed. Elle smiled. Even they had done their part, not moving once.

Will came back, handing the tiny bundle to Sarah. "It's a boy."

Sarah let out a strangled laugh, touching the baby's lips lightly as if she couldn't believe it was real.

Will glanced at his watch. "There's a ferry leaving in a few hours."

Sarah didn't even look up, enamored with her son. "Will, I feel fine."

He squatted down, resting a hand on her shoulder. "Honey, we need to go to the hospital. Just to make sure you are both okay. I'm going to load up the van." Will kissed Sarah on her forehead and stood. "Rest, sweetheart."

Elle looked at Mac. "You aren't going to fly your own sister to the hospital?"

Mac gave her a funny look, his color almost back to normal. "Maybe if I wanted to pop the kid's eardrums. They have to take the ferry."

Her face warmed, and Elle fought the urge to stick her tongue out at him again. How was she supposed to know that? She needed to get out of here before she ruined this heartwarming family moment. "I'll take care of the food."

She busied herself with clearing the table, putting away the leftovers, and cleaning up the kitchen. Will and Mac worked on getting everything ready for the couple to go to Juneau. Every few minutes, one of them would check on Sarah. After a couple of hours, it was time.

Sarah reluctantly passed the baby to Mac. "Can you hold him while I walk to the car?"

"Me?" Mac asked, even though his giant arms already cradled the tiny, blanketed bundle.

Elle's throat closed up. There must be some psychological phenomenon that happened when a man held a baby. Because despite being the singular most infuriating person she had ever met, Mac made a good-looking family man.

Will helped his wife to her feet slowly. "Take your time, sweetheart."

Sarah glanced at the mess she was leaving behind. "Sorry."

"I'll take care of everything here," Elle said with a reassuring smile. "Be safe."

Sarah and Will shuffled out of the room as Mac followed behind with the baby.

Elle stood on the porch and waved goodbye, both exhausted and buzzing with energy at the same time.

The van disappeared down the driveway, and Mac walked back up to the porch.

Elle clasped her hands together as they walked into the lodge. She had just helped bring a baby into the world. A baby! "Can you believe it?"

"Believe what?" Mac didn't even so much as crack a smile.

Elle gaped at him. "We just delivered a baby."

"Actually, I'm pretty sure my sister is the one who delivered the baby. Now we're stuck with the mess and two dogs until they get back."

If Elle hadn't seen him get anxious during the birth, she would almost believe his nonchalant attitude. "Well, I think it's incredible. I don't have any nieces or nephews."

He tilted his head. "No?"

"Only child."

"Ah. So that's the problem."

Elle glared at him. What was that supposed to mean?

Taking a deep breath, she shook it off. "For once, you aren't going to ruin my good mood. I feel amazing about what happened today, and I intend to enjoy it."

Mac lifted an eyebrow. "And what makes you think I don't feel amazing?"

"You're acting like you just mowed the lawn, not like you have a new baby nephew."

"Just because I'm not sitting here bawling doesn't mean I don't have feelings."

Elle bit the inside of her cheek, remembering his poetry and the way he had dried off Dickinson even though he must've been freezing and how he had kissed her until her toes curled. "I know you have feelings."

He pinned her with his gaze. "For example, I feel that I like you a lot. Maybe we should be together."

Her mouth went dry. "But the kiss. You never said anything after."

Mac moved closer, his juniper scent making her light-headed. "On that note, you know what I think we should do right now?" he asked, his voice a husky whisper.

A fire burned in her belly, the promise of a second kiss and more hanging heavy between them. "What?"

He cracked a smile. "I think we should clean up all those nasty blankets."

Elle let out a gasp of exasperation and stomped away. She had never hated Maverick Carter more. Which was really inconvenient because she had never liked him so much either.

CHAPTER TWENTY-THREE

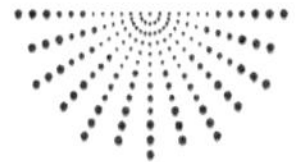

ELLE

Elle flopped back onto the goose-down couch. It was hard to believe that Sarah had given birth right here in this very room earlier today. Although part of the reason that was hard to believe was because they had spent the rest of the day cleaning up, and Elle had the sore body to show for it.

Outside, the sunset cast a warm glow over the island, turning the water a fiery orange. Had it really only been eight days ago that she had first taken in that view? It seemed like a lifetime. Heck, it felt like she had lived a lifetime just today.

Elle yawned into the back of her hand as Mac walked into the room carrying a glass of wine in each hand. He passed one to her. "Hope you're not too tired to celebrate."

She rubbed her forehead with her free hand, her mind as worn-out as her body. "But what about Travis? We were supposed to go get him today."

Mac lifted a shoulder. "It's a bit late for that. If he wants to come back tonight, he knows the way." His mouth quirked up. "And if he shows up, we have enough wine for him too."

Elle held the glass back out to Mac, the idea of sitting here and drinking wine together a little too romantic. Especially when she was torn between hating him and wanting to jump his bones on an hourly basis. "I can't. One of us has to be able to drive back."

"Or you could have a drink with me, and we can spend the night here." He coughed. "Separately, of course."

Her face warmed, and Elle glanced away. She had shared a space with Mac for the past week. There wasn't anything weird about them being alone at the lodge. Especially when there wasn't, and wouldn't ever be, anything going on between them.

Her gaze landed on the dogs curled up in the corner. Dickinson was taking up more than her fair share of Bart's dog bed. "I guess it would be nice for Bart to stay where he's used to."

Mac gave an exaggerated nod. "Exactly. I'm thinking of the dogs."

"Fine, you win." With a laugh, Elle clinked her glass to his. "I thought you didn't like wine."

He looked her in the eye. "But you do."

Elle took a sip, her mouth suddenly dry. How did he do that? How did he always make her feel special? "What varietal is this?"

"Red? That's the kind you like, right?"

Elle bit back a laugh. She'd love to see Mac in LA. He might be the one person on Earth who didn't give a crap what other people thought. "You're right. I like red."

Mac set his wineglass on the coffee table. "I'll go get the bottle for you. I'm going to need more than one glass anyway."

He came back a minute later, handing it to her. "There you go. Its name is Barbara."

Elle giggled. "Barbera."

Mac stuck his tongue out. "Whatever. I told you. I'm a country bumpkin."

She shook her head, setting the bottle aside. For having an Alaska-sized ego, Mac could be oddly hard on himself sometimes. "Well, I like it."

"It's growing on me. The more I drink it, the better it tastes." Mac rubbed his hands together. "How about I build a fire? Keep the wild things away."

Elle swirled her wine, her aching back already feeling better. As long as they were going to stay the night at the lodge, why not enjoy the full experience? That was totally innocent, right? "That'd be nice."

He unbuttoned his cuffs and rolled up his sleeves. Her breath caught, the sight of his muscled arms warming her up more than any fire ever could. Mac had the kind of strength that came with hard work, and something about that turned her knees to mush.

Mac knelt down in front of the fireplace, lighting the kindling before adding a few logs. Once the fire was roaring, he stood and pointed at the couch. "Room on that thing for one more?"

Elle scooted over, hoping she wasn't blushing. She needed to pull herself together. Wasn't it just earlier today she had been reciting all the reasons she had to stay away from him? "Of course."

Mac made his way to the couch and patted a cushion. Both dogs jumped up, making Elle squeal and almost spill her wine.

He rolled his eyes at Dickinson. "Damn dog. I meant Bart."

Elle giggled as she massaged the husky's ears with her free hand. "She doesn't want to be left out."

Mac sat on the other end, scowling as he squeezed between the armrest and the dogs. "Whatever."

Elle scratched Bart's scruffy head next. "Any word from Sarah and Will?"

Mac shook his head. "Just that they got to Juneau safely."

Elle propped her elbow on the back of the couch, resting her temple against her hand. Between the fire and the wine and the cushy couch, she could feel her body relaxing inch by inch. "So are you excited to be an uncle?"

He grinned that gorgeous, genuine smile of his that made her heart skip a beat every time. It was as rare as a sunny day in Darling and just as spectacular. "Thrilled."

Elle couldn't help but smile back. Something about Mac being happy made her happy. Even if he did annoy the heck out of her most of the time. "I hope you're ready when you have kids. You seemed to be in as much pain as Sarah."

"Never speak of that again." Mac shuddered. He looked down at his lap. "Anyway, I don't think that's going to be a problem."

"Why not?"

Mac shrugged. "We've talked about this. The theoretical kids need a theoretical mom. You've been here a week. Come across many single people in town? And it's not like people are champing at the bit to move to Darling."

She frowned. "You're not going to have kids because you really think someone wouldn't want to move to Alaska?"

"It's not about moving here. It's moving here for *me*." His voice cracked, and he looked away.

Elle's heart squeezed. He didn't really believe that, did he? Mac was the total package. He had a huge heart. He was a good person. And if she was being honest with herself, he was gorgeous. What part of that wasn't enough?

But before she could say anything, Mac turned the question back on her. "How about you? Think you'll ever have kids?"

Elle chewed on her lip. She had the same answer to that as she had to everything else. "I don't know."

Mac shook his head. "I used to think I had it bad. Knowing what I wanted and going without. But I actually think you have it worse. You don't know at all."

She winced. Elle knew he didn't mean it to be hurtful, but his words still stung. It wasn't like she wanted to be this way. "It's hard to explain."

Mac held her gaze, his green eyes unblinking. "Try me."

Elle swallowed. Mac had shown her a little bit of his heart. She could do the same. What better place to leave her secrets than in the middle of nowhere with a man she could trust? "I just didn't have a good example. My parents told me they fell in love at first sight, but all I saw was them spending their entire lives fighting. Everything was a struggle. They couldn't even agree on how to raise me."

Mac rested his arm across the back of the couch. "What did they argue about? Big things or little things?"

"Everything." The fire crackled as Elle took a sip of wine. "Like this one time, we went on our first vacation ever. A real vacation, not camping. I was so excited to go on a plane. Anyway, I sat in the middle. There was some really bad turbulence. I started crying, they started yelling, and that's that. I don't remember anything else about the trip."

Elle dropped her head. Even thinking about it made her stomach hurt. "I know that's not that bad in the grand scheme of things. But it pretty much sums up their whole relationship. After that, we never went on another vacation. My mom passed away, and then my dad a little after high school."

Mac shifted on the couch. "So I'm guessing that's where your fear of flying comes from."

Elle looked up as she let out a dry laugh. He never missed a thing. "Yeah."

Mac rested his head against his arm. "I'm sorry, Elle. That had nothing to do with you. But I wish you could have some better memories. You deserve that."

She looked at the fireplace, her chest tight. The logs shifted, and sparks traveled up the river rock chimney. "Don't be. They did one thing right. I wouldn't have this career without them. My mom was a phenomenal cook. She really came alive in the kitchen. That was the only place I ever remember all three of us laughing together."

She turned up the corner of her mouth. When was the last time she had thought about that? After working nonstop for the past eight years, Elle had almost forgotten why she had started in the first place. "Anyway, after they passed, I moved to California and started my social media accounts. I had no idea what it was going to turn into. I just knew that cooking made me happy."

Mac sat up. "Wait a minute. You're not from LA? Then where are you from? Florida?" He shook his head. "No, Texas. I get the feeling you'd love to kick me in the ass with some spurs."

Elle burst out laughing. Mac made her furious enough to scream, but no one had ever made her laugh like him either. "As tempting as that is sometimes, no. Neither."

Mac squinted at her. "Where, then?"

"I'll never tell." She flashed him a teasing smile, knowing it would drive him crazy not to know and relishing the chance to push his buttons for a change. "Your turn. Did you grow up here? In Darling?"

Mac gestured to the room. "Right here at the lodge."

"I can't imagine growing up in a hotel. That must've been fun."

"Tell that to childhood me, constantly doing chores around this place," Mac muttered. He quirked an eyebrow. "Want to see my old room?"

"Are you kidding? Of course." Elle set her wine on the side table, standing from the couch. She couldn't resist the chance to find out more about Mac. For being a grump who lived on an island, he was full of surprises.

The dogs barely lifted their heads as she and Mac headed upstairs. They walked to the end of the hallway, and Mac opened the door for her. "Brace yourself. It's not the executive suite you're used to."

Elle stepped inside. While definitely small, the room was neat and simple. It kind of reminded Elle of Mac's shop in a way. "Did you like it? Living here as a kid?"

"I'm still here, aren't I?"

Her gaze darted away. Once again, Mac showing her a glimpse of his heart lowered the walls around her own. "Yes, but are you sure you're not just afraid?"

Mac shifted his feet. "What the hell would I be afraid of?"

"Well, you've always been here. Always known this place. You say you love it, but what if you've just convinced yourself of that? What if you're afraid to try something else? Even if you really, really want to."

Mac cleared his throat. "Are you sure we're still talking about me?"

She turned to face him, and her nose almost touched his chest. She could feel heat radiating off him, his juniper scent beckoning her closer.

Her heart slammed into her ribs. Elle could've made a million excuses. It was the excitement of the moment, the complete and total high of helping deliver a baby and doing something that actually mattered. It was this place, Alaska, and all that time they'd spent together that made her do crazy things. Or maybe it was the wine that made her crave closeness. Heck, she could blame it on the small room, that there was no space between them.

None of them were the truth. The truth was she wanted this. She wanted Mac.

"I don't know about all that." Mac gently tucked a strand of hair behind her ear, looking at her like she was the most important thing in the world. "But there is something I have been meaning to tell you."

Elle licked her lips, her body tingling from his touch. "What's that?"

"The poem was about you," he said, his voice husky. "It's always been about you."

That was everything she needed to hear.

Elle threw her arms around his neck, and Mac held her close, whispering her name. He lowered his head to hers, and she stood on her tiptoes to meet him halfway.

Elle melted into the kiss, into him. She had a million reasons not to do it and only one reason to. But that singular reason was the only one that mattered.

It was hard to ignore the truth from an honest man.

CHAPTER TWENTY-FOUR

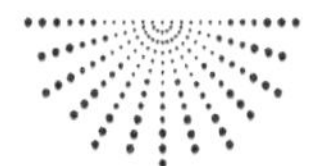

MAC

Mac shifted in the bed, keeping his eyes closed just a bit longer. He didn't need an alarm clock to know it was five in the morning. He always woke up at the same time every day, no matter what he had done the day before or how much he had drunk.

He stretched his arms overhead but was stopped short by the wall. Mac felt around with his big toe and found another wall. He blinked his eyes open as he remembered why there seemed to be no space. For one, he was in the smallest room in the lodge. For two, Elle was squeezed in bed next to him.

Mac's body felt warm at the memory of last night. The small room hadn't been a problem then. In fact, they couldn't seem to get close enough.

He slowly turned to his side and looked at Elle. She still slept, her blonde hair flopped every which way and her face scrunched up on one side where it smooshed against the pillow.

His breath hitched. She was perfect.

Mac stayed there for a few more minutes, wanting to soak up every drop of this moment. Hell, he could lie here all day.

It felt weird in a way to know there were no guests at the lodge to think about. Mac had been working this time of year since he had been old enough to see over the kitchen counters. But of course, his sister had never had a baby before.

His cheeks burned at the memory of how he'd acted when Sarah went into labor. Thank goodness there hadn't been many witnesses. Elle was right. He'd have to be careful if he ever had a child of his own. Lord only knows how he might behave then.

His heart squeezed. His own child. Mac always kept himself safely distanced from that dream. He couldn't have a family without a wife. And no woman could live the way he did.

Except maybe for one.

Elle had made it clear from the beginning that Alaska wasn't her favorite place on Earth. But after last night, Mac didn't know if he could live with himself if he let her leave without at least asking her to stay.

There was always the chance that Elle would laugh in his face, return to California, and never look back.

But there was another possibility. One that made his heart go soft like butter on a hot flapjack. The small, tiniest, most hopeless possibility that this life was the one Elle wanted. That Mac was the one she wanted.

A whine came from outside the door. Mac eased himself out of bed, gently tucking the quilt back around Elle. He pulled on yesterday's clothes and crept out of the room.

Dickinson and Bart waited for him in the hallway, tails wagging.

Mac gave the husky the stink eye, making it clear that

talking wasn't welcome at this hour. The three of them headed downstairs, where Mac started the coffee maker before letting the dogs outside.

As he watched them sniff around, Mac again wondered about upgrading his home. What would Elle want? A big kitchen, maybe? She loved cooking and was good at it. Mac rested a hand on his stomach, convinced he had gained at least five pounds since Elle had moved into his shop.

Mac scratched his beard. Will had had his own construction company before moving to Darling. Maybe Mac could run the idea by him once they were back from Juneau and had a chance to settle in. Mac wanted to make sure it was possible before promising Elle anything.

Because in this moment, he'd promise her anything she desired to get her to stay.

He whistled, and the dogs trotted back inside the house. Mac poured himself a cup of coffee and decided to tidy up a bit while Elle slept. They had done the majority of the cleaning last night, but Mac wanted the lodge to be perfect when Sarah got home. She would have enough to do without picking up after them.

Mac made his way to the sitting room, where the fire from last night had long since burned out. Setting his coffee aside, Mac shoveled out the ashes and dumped them in the pail.

A buzzing sound started in his ear, and Mac shook his head. Shit, was his hearing going bad already? He was always careful with ear protection on his flights, but that didn't guard him against getting older.

The buzzing stopped, and Mac put the lid on the ash pail, dusting his hands. He walked back over to the coffee table to grab his cup.

Mac tilted his head. The buzzing was back, louder this time. And it wasn't coming from inside his head.

He followed the sound to the side of the couch where Elle had sat last night. He picked up the cushion, and her phone tumbled to the floor.

Mac scooped it up, noticing the battery was low. As far as the messages that covered the screen, he turned a blind eye to those. That was Elle's business.

He made his way to the kitchen. Maybe there was a spare charger in the junk drawer. If not, he'd check the office.

Mac didn't find anything, and the phone never stopped buzzing. Now he was starting to get worried. What the hell was so important? Did someone die or something?

He chewed the inside of his cheek. This might be an exception to his privacy policy. If he couldn't find a charger, he at least wanted to pass on the news to Elle before her phone shut off.

Mac scrolled past the missed calls, trying to piece together what was going on from the texts. They were all from the same lady, asking about a TV show and a plan to come home and being back in two days *or else*.

His stomach sank. The TV show. The TV show that Elle had told him about. The one where they would replace her if she wasn't back in five days. And that was three days ago.

Mac rubbed the back of his neck. What the hell was he supposed to do now? He didn't want to tell her he had looked at her phone. He didn't want to talk about it at all.

But Elle deserved this show. She had worked hard. And more than that, he now knew that cooking was the one good, tenuous connection she had with her parents.

Mac let out a shaky breath. Goddammit. He couldn't let her go back without saying something. But Mac couldn't ask her to choose either. Did he really think that a new kitchen could replace her entire life back in LA? That he was worth giving all that up for? Hell, Mac wouldn't even choose himself.

He swallowed. But Elle had confessed she didn't know if she liked her work anymore. If only he knew how much the show really meant to her.

Except there was no way to ask her without showing his hand. Elle never let him get away with anything, and she'd pry the truth out of him.

But there was one person on this island who knew all about the life waiting for Elle in California.

Mac's body turned cold as he realized what he had to do. He had to break his cardinal rule of respecting privacy for a second time that morning. Mac needed answers only someone else could give.

He filled a thermos, scribbled a note for Elle, and grabbed the keys to his truck.

As he drove, Mac took a drink from his thermos, wincing as the hot coffee stung his tongue. He needed the fortification because he was about to do something he swore he never would. Mac was going to put his heart on the line.

* * *

HE WAS RIGHT where Natasha said he would be. The damn fool had traveled to the south side of the island. This whole time, Mac and Elle had been looking in the exact wrong spot.

As he surveyed the site, Mac was almost impressed. Travis had fashioned himself a small shelter that looked like it would at least keep him dry.

He watched the area for a few minutes, waiting to catch sight of Travis. Mac didn't want to go poking around the camp uninvited. For all he knew, Travis would think Mac was a bear, and he probably had a gun. The last thing Mac needed right now was to get popped in the ass.

After a few minutes, Travis stepped from the tent.

Mac's jaw dropped. The easygoing guy from the

Ketchikan airport looked like a different person. A thick, unkempt beard covered Travis's face. His hair had grown longer, curling over the edge of his collar. He hadn't been big when Mac met him, but Travis was a twig of a stick now.

Holy shit. It had barely been more than a week. But the kid looked like he had been sucking on rocks and rainwater since he disappeared. Apparently, it hadn't occurred to Travis to buy some actual food when he bought all this other crap.

Mac rustled some tree branches and cleared his throat. Travis looked up, his eyes searching in his direction. Mac made his way towards the site slowly. He didn't want to scare the life out of the dummy because, by the looks of things, he wasn't sure how much life Travis had left.

His eyes widened when Mac stepped out of the cover of the forest. "Mac? How did you find me?"

Mac shrugged. "Got help. Tried to do it on our own, but that didn't work."

Travis nodded. "I remember hearing you and Elle calling my name."

"Why didn't you answer, then? You don't like your ex-girlfriend or something?"

"Ex-fiancé," Travis corrected him, though it probably sounded as empty to him as it did to Mac. "It's not that. I knew she would convince me to come home."

"Look, this sounds like this is going to take a minute, and I have my own agenda." Mac held up the thermos. "Mind if I join you? I brought coffee."

Travis licked his lips. "Coffee?"

With a sigh, Mac stepped forward and passed him the cup. "Careful. It's hot."

"I miss coffee." Travis wrapped his hands around the thermos, looking down at it like Mac had handed him a gold bar.

Mac shoved his hands in his pockets. The morning air

was brisk, and he had a feeling he wasn't going to get his hand warmer back anytime soon. "What's the problem with going back? Doesn't seem like such a terrible life, from the sounds of it."

"You're right. But I screwed up big-time." Travis dropped his chin to his chest. "Elle probably hates me."

Mac's stomach twisted. "Because you dumped her?"

"No, not that. Elle and I were really more like friends, anyway." Travis took a sip of coffee and then another. "Because of her job. I don't think Elle really likes what she does, but it was going to change, or at least that's what she thought. She got an offer for a miniseries. It would be more work at first, but with the income from the merchandise and everything, Elle was hoping it meant she could finally slow down a little. Have more time for the stuff she actually cared about."

Mac's throat tightened. Well, shit. He had come here to get an answer. He had just been hoping it was different. "Sounds pretty good. I bet she'll be great at it."

Travis ran his hand through his greasy hair. "Yeah, if I hadn't screwed it up."

Mac dragged the toe of his boot through the dirt. "What does you running off to commune with nature have to do with Elle's TV show?"

Travis rubbed his forehead. "The whole thing was based around us as a couple. I mean, a lot of it would be Elle in the kitchen. But they wanted to see us go on dates, plan the wedding. Stuff like that. That's what sold them. The lifestyle angle."

Mac sucked in a breath, trying not to be sick right there in the forest. He hadn't known that part, and Elle hadn't told him. Even if he had known, what difference would it make? It wasn't like people wouldn't notice that Travis had suddenly been replaced by a guy twice his size with no patience for bullshit. "I'm beginning to see the problem."

Travis's shoulders slumped. "Elle did so much for me, and all I had to do was be there. We weren't in love, but I do care about her. I'd do anything to make it up to her. To be the man she needed."

He shook his head, looking at Mac. "I'm sorry. What did you want to talk about again?"

Mac swallowed, willing his voice not to crack. "It's not important." With a deep breath, he straightened. "Look. You can't sit here forever. Well, you could, but you'd die. Alaskan winter isn't friendly to camping." His hands shook, and Mac shoved them deeper into his pockets. "But Elle is still in Darling right now if you want to give her the same speech you just gave me. My recommendation is to make choices you can live with."

Travis sat up, his eyes brighter. "Do you really think I have a chance?"

For a moment, Mac wasn't there. He was back with Elle. Her secrets were only for him. It was a gift and a curse that she was the one woman he would never forget.

His heart cracked in half. That's what he got for wanting more. But Mac loved Elle too much to ask her to choose him. He didn't know what scared him more. That he might take her away from something wonderful or that she might choose that on her own.

But he could at least keep his word. Elle had wanted Travis back and life to be normal again? Mac would make that happen. After all, he always kept his promises.

He looked Travis in the eye. "Better yet, I'll help you."

CHAPTER TWENTY-FIVE

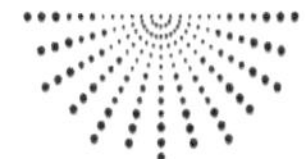

ELLE

It felt delicious to wake up without an alarm. Elle burrowed into the blankets, wishing she could stay in this moment forever. She let out a sigh, the lingering juniper scent taking her back to last night.

Her heart stretched in her chest. Elle had always done everything to protect herself from heartbreak. Where had that gotten her? A career that sucked out her soul? Lonely in a world where she was never alone? A life she didn't even want to go back to?

Then, the least likely person on the planet turned it all around. Mac could rile her up like no one else, but at the same time, he was the only one who saw her for who she really was.

Elle blinked her eyes open. Daylight lit up the room. Mac had probably gotten up hours ago. He never slept in.

As much as Elle wanted to lie here all day, she should get up too. Real life didn't stop just because she was on cloud nine. Will and Sarah would be home eventually. Mac probably had flights scheduled. They had to find Travis.

Elle swallowed. Most importantly, she had to make a choice. She wasn't ready to walk away from everything yet, but she could at least give her and Mac a chance.

Her stomach fluttered with the promise of more wonderful moments. She rested a hand on her tummy, and it took her a minute to realize what that unfamiliar feeling was.

Hope.

Hope that things could be better. Hope that whatever was going on between her and Mac could last more than a week. Hope that maybe her entire life fell apart so that something else could fall back together.

Elle reached for her phone, but her fingers brushed against smooth wood. She pushed herself up on her elbows to peek at the nightstand.

No phone.

She frowned. Had she left it downstairs? Elle couldn't remember the last time she'd lost track of her phone. But then again, she'd never fallen in love before either.

Elle bit her lip, waiting for the tight feeling in her stomach. It never came.

But you have met the man you will marry.

She stepped out of bed, shivering as she plucked her clothes from the floor and dressed. Even though they had crept a week closer to summer, it didn't feel any warmer. Was this something she could get used to again?

Her pulse quickened. She was going to find out.

As soon as Elle stepped out of the bedroom, the dogs came running and greeted her with wagging tails. She giggled, giving them each an equal number of scratches. Elle had dreaded the idea of saying goodbye to the husky. Maybe she wouldn't ever have to.

She made her way downstairs, the scent of freshly brewed

coffee luring her into the kitchen. Next to the coffee machine, her phone sat with a note under it.

GOOD MORNING. COFFEE IS READY. BE BACK SOON. -MAC.

AT THE BOTTOM, Mac had drawn a heart. Or at least Elle assumed that's what it was supposed to be. It looked more like a spiky triangle.

She smiled to herself. After years of not knowing what she wanted, she had never been so certain. Now that she had finally decided, she didn't want to waste another minute.

Elle poured herself a cup of coffee and scooped up her phone. The battery was almost dead, and it was easy to see why. Eight missed calls and fifteen texts from her manager.

As she scrolled through the texts, the familiar tight feeling crept back into her chest. Elle didn't need to listen to the voicemails to guess those were all about the miniseries too.

This was how it would always be with her career. She could work twenty-four hours a day, and it wouldn't be enough. *She* wouldn't be enough.

For so long, Elle had thought she could force herself to keep going, to try harder, to do more. That if she worked hard enough, she would be allowed to be happy. Until she realized that she didn't have to.

Elle leaned against the kitchen island and tapped on the phone screen. Hopefully, the battery lasted long enough for her to change her life.

Lacey picked up on the first ring. "Finally. You forgot to send me your flight info. When will you be back?"

Elle took a deep breath. She could do this. She had done hard things before. The only difference this time was that she was doing it to be happy. "I don't know. I'm not ready to come back yet."

"What am I supposed to do with that info?" Lacey snapped. "I hope you realize what you're doing. People like the Alaska stuff now, but that won't last forever."

Elle's stomach knotted up. She closed her eyes, remembering the way Mac had looked at her last night. That he actually cared about who she was, not just what she was. "I'm going to keep posting. I just don't know when I'll be back."

"You realize I worked a miracle, right? They're willing to work around the whole Travis thing, figure out another angle." Lacey blew air into the phone. "I guess we can slap someone else's name on the cookbook if it comes down to it."

Elle winced. Lacey's words stung, but that was exactly what Elle needed to hear. She needed the reminder that she was just an interchangeable piece to them. But Elle only had this one life, and she couldn't swap out her memories at the end of the day. "I'm sorry. I'll let you know if anything changes."

They hung up, and Elle waited for the panic to settle in. For the heaviness that meant she had failed, that she hadn't tried hard enough.

But instead, she felt truly awake for the first time in years. And when Elle thought about the look on Mac's face when she told him? She wanted to squeal. He'd be so proud of her. More importantly, she was proud of herself.

Elle practically skipped as she carried her coffee to the living room. The dogs followed her, their nails clicking against the hardwood floors.

She paused at the window with her favorite view. Outside, the water sparkled in the morning sun, and even the forest looked greener. A bald eagle enjoyed the rare clear day from its perch in a treetop.

Her first few days in Darling, Elle had thought the weather was miserable. But she had learned that same miserable weather made a person appreciate the nice days so much more. And after spending the last eight years being able to enjoy nothing, she was ready for the sunshine.

Elle had just set her coffee down and settled onto the couch when the dogs jumped up and ran from the room. A door closed. "Elle?"

She jumped up and headed towards the front door. She couldn't wait to tell Mac. "I'm here!"

He met her halfway in the kitchen, and her breath caught. How was it possible she liked him even more this morning?

Elle placed a hand on her hip. "I hope you weren't trying to ditch me. Or did you forget I know where you live?"

His mouth quirked up. "I wouldn't dream of it. Even if I moved, you'd just track me down."

"You know me so well." She giggled. "I'm glad you're back. I have something to tell you."

"So do I." Mac shifted his feet. "I went to find Travis."

Elle blinked at him. Maybe she needed more coffee. Did he say what she thought he had said? "What? You went without me?

"I didn't want to wake you up." Mac rubbed the back of his neck, glancing away. "Will called this morning. They're coming back today. I thought I'd go get Travis to get him on a plane out of here as soon as possible. There aren't other places to stay besides the lodge."

"Oh. That makes sense." Elle twisted her hands. She had imagined this morning going a lot differently than talking about her ex-fiancé. But she hadn't known that Will and Sarah were coming back so soon. And Travis needed to be found. Who knew what kind of shape the poor guy was in? Elle glanced over Mac's shoulder. "So where is he?"

Mac sighed. "He wasn't there. Natasha was wrong."

Her stomach sank. If Natasha had been wrong about that, what if she had been wrong about everything?

Elle shook it off. That didn't change a thing. She had made her decision, and she wasn't changing her mind because some kooky woman in the forest wasn't psychic after all. "So we'll just keep looking on our own again."

"I guess so." Mac ran his hand through his hair. "But I think we should take it easy for now. We both need rest after the past few days. We'll start looking again tomorrow after we bring Bart back over."

Elle nodded. Mac was right, even though rest was the last thing on her mind. But it's not like she and Mac were on their honeymoon. Although a honeymoon with Mac sounded like a lot of fun. "Good idea."

Mac held her gaze, his eyes turned down. She knitted her brows together. Was there something he wasn't telling her? "Everything okay?"

"Everything is perfect." He gave her a small smile. "Just thinking how nice it is to be here with you."

She stood on her tiptoes, giving him a kiss. "Then we'll have to do it again sometime."

Elle stepped back, and she swore his eyes glistened. For being a man who claimed he had no feelings, he could sure be emotional. Then again, like Mac said, the past couple of days had been exhausting. Maybe he was more worn-out than she realized.

Mac cleared his throat. "You said you had something to tell me?"

She chewed on the inside of her cheek. Mac had just become an uncle yesterday, and he'd barely had a chance to enjoy it. Maybe she should keep her news to herself for just a little longer. She would tell him about the miniseries later, after Will and Sarah got back. "You know what? It slipped my mind."

After all, it wasn't like one day would change anything.

CHAPTER TWENTY-SIX

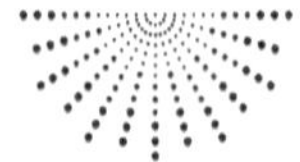

ELLE

Elle hummed to herself as she brushed her hair. As soon as Mac was back, she would tell him everything.

That she wanted this if he wanted it too.

That she had no idea what she was doing.

And that it didn't scare her at all because she loved him.

Her breath hitched. Yes, she loved him. So what if Natasha had been wrong about Travis? Elle didn't need a psychic to know how she felt. Now that she knew what she wanted, nothing was going to change that.

Dickinson let out a whine and ran to the door. Elle set the brush down, smiling to herself. Mac must be home. Will and Sarah had returned on the morning ferry, and Mac had taken Bart over to the lodge afterwards. Waiting for him to get back had been both the longest and shortest hour of her life.

A knock came at the door, and Elle frowned. Why was Mac knocking at his own shop? He normally just barged in and started cursing.

Another knock. She shook her head. Maybe it was someone from town.

Elle walked over, opening the door. Her jaw dropped when she saw who stood on the other side. "Travis?"

Her chest tightened. Just behind Travis stood Mac, a blank expression on his face. What in the world was going on?

Travis gave her his usual lazy smile. "Hey, babe. I'm ready to go home."

She felt light-headed. This must be some bizarre parallel universe. That was the only explanation. They had driven through a portal or something on their way home yesterday. Travis had broken up with her, and after a week of looking for him, he just showed up at Mac's shop, acting like nothing happened? That didn't make any sense. "Uh, okay. So go home."

"I mean, go home with you." He stepped closer, taking her hands in his. "I know I screwed up. But I'll find a way to make it up to you. I'll have my dad talk to the producer for the miniseries. We'll get everything smoothed out. I promise, things will be exactly the same."

Elle jerked her hands back, her heart pounding. She had thought Travis had totally lost it when he first ran off into the forest. That had been nothing compared to this. "Are you joking? You were the one who told me you can't live a lie. And you were right. We aren't in love, Travis. You can't honestly want to go back to that."

His face strained. "Please. Whatever it takes, we can fix this."

Her stomach churned, and she glanced at Mac. Why was he just standing there, acting like nothing was going on? She swallowed. Unless this wasn't a surprise to him. Elle brushed past Travis as she stepped out into the gray day. "If you'll excuse me for a minute."

Travis called after her, but she ignored him. Elle stomped over to Mac, grabbing his hand. "I need to talk to you."

Mac followed her silently to the dock. As they walked, a few stray raindrops fell from the sky and dotted the ground.

Once they were out of earshot of Travis, she let go of Mac's hand and faced him. Elle took a deep breath, trying to keep her voice from shaking. "I'm so confused right now. Please help me be less confused."

He blinked at her, the rain falling faster now. "I don't get the problem. This is what you wanted."

Elle reeled. She couldn't have been more shocked if he had dumped a bucket of ice water over her head. "What the hell are you talking about?"

Mac tilted his head, his gaze steely. "Now I'm confused. You don't remember invading my space and demanding I get Travis back?"

Her stomach sank. This wasn't happening. Had she just imagined last night? The whole week? "Are you serious? Everything has changed since then!"

His face hardened. "Has it? I am a pilot who lives on an island. You're a celebrity from LA. You have internet search results, for Christ's sake. There are no TV shows here, Elle. This isn't where you belong."

Her throat grew tight. She hadn't even gotten to tell him yet that she turned down the miniseries. And now, there didn't seem to be a point. "This is what you want? For me to go back?"

Mac folded his arms, blocking her out. "Why else do you think I brought Travis here?"

Her eyes burned. As much as Elle hated flying, she couldn't stand to be here one minute longer than necessary. "Then you better make an opening in your schedule for two right now."

Mac gave a firm nod, his hair turning darker with each raindrop. "You're going back with him. Good."

"Good?" She scoffed, her vision blurring. "All you can say is good?"

He scowled. "I don't know what you're so upset about. I kept my promise. You wanted me to get Travis and send you back to LA. Well, sweetheart, that's what's happening."

A sob clawed at her. It wasn't that she wouldn't have a chance to say goodbye to Sarah or that she had passed on the miniseries when she could've done it after all. It was that she had been willing to give it all up for Mac, but he wasn't even willing to fight for her. "You lied to me."

Mac didn't even flinch. Who was this stranger? Where was the guy who wrote poetry and took in stray dogs? "About Sarah and Will coming back? I had to give Travis a chance to get cleaned up. He looked like he had been on some kind of survival mission, and not a very successful one at that."

"No." Her chest tightened as her heart shrunk into a pinpoint. "You lied about what Natasha said. She was right. She knew where Travis was."

Mac shrugged, his expression colder than the Alaskan sea. "So? That changes nothing."

A chill ran down her back, but it had nothing to do with the rain that drenched her clothes. She had it all wrong. This was Alaska. Sunny days didn't last forever. "It changes everything."

CHAPTER TWENTY-SEVEN

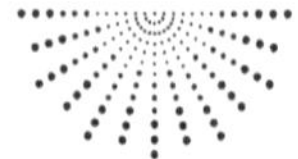

MAC

Mac took a tentative sip of his coffee, barely resisting the urge to spit it out right there on the shop floor. He poured the cup down the drain. "Damn that woman."

Elle had ruined everything.

Before she had come around, Mac had been fine with crappy coffee and canned soup and being alone. He was determined to get back to that point.

His eyes prickled, and he blinked furiously, refusing to cry. Mac had done the right thing, taking Elle home. Her life in LA wasn't perfect, but it was still better than what he could offer her. Even if he had asked her to stay, it wouldn't have taken her long to figure that out on her own. Her leaving Darling was inevitable.

If only doing the right thing didn't break his heart in half. Mac had seen it coming from a thousand miles away. He had known all along that to live this kind of life, the life he loved, he had to be single. But knowing that didn't make it hurt any less.

His throat tightened, remembering the way Elle had looked at him as she walked off his plane. She hadn't said a thing, and neither had he. They hadn't needed to. Because they both knew that nothing, no explanation, would be enough to change anything. It wasn't meant to be.

Mac took a deep breath. It was well past time to get back to real life. Not just real life. His old life. The one without Elle.

He rubbed his eyes before checking the time. The Driftwood Coffee Company would be open for another hour. If he was going to finally pull himself back together, a decent cup of coffee seemed like a good place to start.

Mac whistled to the husky. "Come on, girl."

He made a point of taking the dog with him everywhere, not that he could've stopped her if he tried. No one had claimed her yet, and Mac had reluctantly accepted that he now had a husky. Although if someone had stepped forward, Mac didn't know how he'd handle both the loss of Dickinson and the last connection he had with Elle.

But Mac hated leaving her alone when he was gone on flights. Something else that was different from when Elle had been there. Dickinson lost her mind every time Mac got home from work, and he felt like the meanest man on the planet leaving her. So he spent as much time with her as he could.

Mac shoved his hands in his pockets, the fine mist sticking to his beard as they walked to the coffee shop. It was a month closer to summer, but the day was as cold as his heart.

His phone rang, and Mac let out a groan when he glanced at the screen. "What's up, Sarah?"

"A little sister can't call her big brother for no reason?" she asked sweetly.

Mac grunted. "Maybe some sisters. Not you."

She cleared her throat. "I just wanted to see how you're doing. I've barely seen you since we got back from the hospital."

Mac worked his jaw, knowing what she really meant was she hadn't seen him much since Elle had left. He hated the pity in Sarah's voice. Made him sick. She had a newborn she should be worried about, but instead, Mac was the big baby in her life. "I'm fine."

"Yeah, you sound like it." Sarah let out a huff. "What are you up to?"

Mac turned the corner, heading up Main Street. "Going to get some coffee from Grace's shop."

"Oh, want to bring me a latte? I'm trying to catch up after not being able to have any for nine months."

His shoulders pinched together. "I don't really have time."

Even though he had nothing else to do today except lick his wounds. It was a struggle keeping busy, especially with the lodge closed for summer. But he didn't want to be around anyone right now. Definitely not Sarah. She'd take one look at him and see the truth written all over his face.

"Don't have time to visit your nephew? He's not going to know who his Uncle Mac is at this rate."

Mac looked up at the gray sky. He might be heartbroken, but he wasn't heartless. Mac loved the little guy. "Fine. I'll get your damn latte."

He ended the call, walking into the Driftwood Coffee Company while the dog waited for him outside. "Can I get a latte for Sarah in a to-go cup, please, and a bag of the house blend for me?"

Grace reached for the coffee. "Whole bean or ground?"

He gritted his teeth. There it was again. A reminder his life had been invaded. "What did Elle order?"

He hoped it sounded casual, but based on the tightness of his jaw, he doubted it.

Grace opened the bag. "Ground. I remember her saying that you'd need to buy a grinder so that you can make it fresh each morning."

He scowled. "Well, she's not here anymore, and that sounds like a pain in the ass."

"Jesus, Mac. You asked a question, and I answered."

The anger was sucked out of him, and he felt two inches tall. Just because he was dying on the inside, it wasn't an excuse to be a jerk. "Sorry. I haven't been sleeping much."

She gave him a look. "I can tell."

Mercifully, she left it at that. His shoulders sagged. Mac wasn't in the mood to talk about his feelings, and Grace probably wasn't in the mood to talk to him either after he snapped at her.

She poured the beans into the grinder before starting on the latte. Once the grinder kicked off, Grace handed him the resealed bag, along with Sarah's latte. "Did you need anything else?"

Mac eyed the pastry case. He hadn't had much of an appetite since Elle had left. That probably wasn't helping his disposition either. But he always had a weakness for cherry danish. "No, thanks. I'm good."

Grace nabbed the danish with the tongs, slipping it into a paper sleeve and handing it to Mac. "On the house. Enjoy."

Mac shook his head, holding the pastry back out to her. "I don't need it."

"So? Do you want it?"

It's okay to have what you want.

Mac's throat closed up. He needed to get out of here. He paid for the beans and the latte before gathering everything up and heading outside. "Thank you."

Balancing the beans and latte in one arm, Mac took a bite of the cherry danish with the other. As they walked back to the shop, Dickinson miraculously managed to keep up and beg at the same time.

Mac swallowed. What did he want?

For the longest time, Mac had told himself that he had everything he needed. But things had changed. He knew better now. He had gotten a taste of that other life, and he was hungry for more. But what was the point of wanting something if it could never happen?

Back at the shop, Mac tossed the paper sleeve and left the bag of coffee on the kitchen counter. Then, he and Dickinson climbed into the cab of his truck. Mac had thought hell would freeze over before he treated the dog like a person. But he had gotten used to riding with someone, and he liked it.

They drove out to the lodge, the forest whizzing past him in a green blur. These were the moments when his mind would wander, taking the bit in its mouth and pulling the reins from his hand. Mac let it.

Time seemed to stop as he remembered the best, worst week of his life. He saw Elle's smile, so rare in the beginning. How good it felt when he earned it. Her sunshine hair and blue, blue eyes. How she made everything seem possible.

His chest tightened. Every memory was salt in a wound. Every memory was a heartbeat that kept him alive.

As Mac tore down the gravel road, he glimpsed a doe directly in his path. He slammed on the brakes, praying both not to hit the deer and that the awful racket his truck was making wasn't something serious. Dickinson flattened herself against the seat, whining. The coffee shifted in the cup holder, and white foam sloshed out.

The old truck skidded to a stop just inches from the deer. His heart pounded. Mac could see the amber color of her eyes as she stood there, frozen. A moment later, two fawns made their way out of the forest, taking careful steps on gangly legs. Once their spotted hinds had disappeared into the forest trees, the doe left her post and joined them in three quick leaps.

Mac sucked in shallow breaths. He gave Dickinson a reassuring pat before righting the coffee. Mac put the truck into drive, relieved it seemed to be working. Darling might be small, but it wasn't a good idea to stay parked in the middle of a road where the only thing that kept people from going a hundred miles an hour was the occasional pothole.

The sweat that covered his body turned cold. Mac had only had one true accident ever. He remembered Elle swimming out to him, looking like a drowned rat. The damn dog had been right there beside her.

Despite the icy water, Mac had felt warm to his toes. This woman, this delicate orchid, had jumped into the Alaskan sea to come to his rescue. She had put her own safety on the line for him.

His heart sank. And Mac had just let her get on that plane and walk away.

The sign for the lodge came into view, growing large. Mac tightened his grip on the steering wheel, whizzing past it. Sarah would understand.

It's okay to have what you want.

The only question was, did what he want also want him?

CHAPTER TWENTY-EIGHT

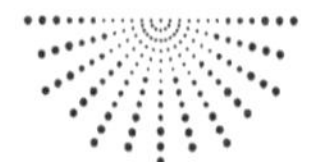

MAC

Mac bumped along the dirt road, easing his foot off the gas when he glimpsed a flash of white. He shifted in his seat, driving a bit closer to the trailer before slowing to a stop.

Natasha sat in one of the folding chairs outside. She didn't look the least bit surprised to see him. In fact, she looked damn pleased with herself.

A shiver traveled down his spine. That only turned up the dial on his heebie-jeebies. He wasn't sure how Natasha's vision actually worked, but hopefully, it didn't zone in on pathetic and heartbroken bachelors.

Leaving Dickinson in the cab with the windows cracked, Mac stepped out of the truck and slammed the door. He walked up to Natasha. "I have a bone to pick with you."

She gave him a patient smile. "I know."

Mac's body was overheated despite the chilly mist that drifted down from the gray sky. "Elle and Travis went back. So then what was that about? That crap that I can have what I want?"

Natasha sighed, as if he were the problem. "You didn't listen, Maverick. My request was very simple."

Mac gritted his teeth. Nothing was ever simple with Natasha. Most of the time, he didn't even know what she was talking about. "No, it wasn't. Because I can want someone all day long, but it doesn't mean she wants me too."

Natasha turned her gaze up towards the canopy. "You know what I was thinking about just now?"

"What?" His money was on ways to annoy the crap out of him.

Natasha looked at him again, leaning back in the chair. "How much we have in common."

He barked a laugh. She had to be two feet shorter than him, even when she was standing, and weighed a fraction of what he did. Not to mention the age difference. And, oh yeah, the fact that she was supposedly psychic. The only magic Mac enjoyed was in fiction novels. What could they possibly have in common? "I have to disagree."

Natasha shook her head, her friendly expression gone. That freaked Mac out even more. "I want you to be right. I think we shouldn't have anything in common. I know why I keep to myself. My husband is gone. So are both of my children. I risked my heart, and now I have the scars to show for it. Where are your scars?"

He gulped. She might as well call him a chicken for what it was worth. "I don't need to burn myself to know the stove is hot."

Natasha folded her hands in her lap. "Being hurt is better than feeling nothing at all."

Mac pressed his lips together. She was wrong. If it was better, he wouldn't be here right now. He wouldn't be desperate to make the pain go away so he could go on with life. He wouldn't be terrified about losing the memories when he did move on. "You know what? Forget it. I'll see you later."

She nodded, even though they both knew that the chance of running into each other was about as slim as a sunny day in Alaska. "Mac?"

His shoulders tensed. What more could she possibly have to say? Mac had come here for answers, but he was leaving only more confused and pissed off to boot. "What?"

A shadow passed across Natasha's face. "I'm not going to tell you again. Don't wait for someone else's permission to be happy. We only get to do this once."

She stood and glided inside the trailer, leaving Mac working his mouth like a fish out of water.

He should've never listened to Natasha in the first place. All she did was get his hopes up for nothing.

Mac swallowed. But Natasha wasn't the one he needed an answer from.

He had begged Elle to tell him what she wanted. Now he realized he had been asking the wrong question the whole time.

His heart squeezed. After all, what good was knowing what he wanted if he didn't ask for it?

* * *

MAC FOUND Sarah in the sitting room, curled up on the couch with the baby. The husky trotted in behind him, joining Bart on the dog bed.

She smiled, reaching for the coffee. "You're an angel." Her eyes narrowed as she took him in. "A tired angel."

Mac shrugged. That was the least of his problems right now. "No more tired than you, I'm sure."

Sarah took a gulp of coffee and set the cup aside. "On that

note, do you mind holding Billy while I take a quick bathroom break?"

She stood and passed the blanketed bundle to Mac. Once Sarah's back was turned, Mac stuck his tongue out and made a face. The baby gave him a toothless smile.

His chest tightened. What was it like to have all this? That he didn't know. What he did know was that there was only one person he wanted to have it with.

Sarah came back into the room and reached for the baby, but Mac pulled Billy closer. "Mind if I hold him for a minute?"

She smirked. "Be my guest. You can change the dirty diapers too."

"No, thank you." Mac scowled. "So how are things? Minus the diapers."

She took a seat and reached for her coffee again. "Oh, fine. I still feel a little guilty taking the summer off. We've already had reservation requests for next year."

Mac bounced Billy gently, not quite ready to talk about his own stuff yet. "There's nothing to feel guilty about. You had a baby."

"Must be a family curse. Speaking of people who took the summer off, Mom and Dad called me earlier this morning." Sarah shook her head. "Now that I had Billy, they're counting down the days until they get home. They feel awful for booking the trip when they did."

Mac snorted, and Billy stared at him. "You're right. Must be a curse."

Sarah took another gulp of coffee. "This is actual heaven, even if it's cold." She eyed him. "Not that I'm complaining about getting coffee delivered or anything, but is there any reason why it took you an hour to get here from town?"

Mac swallowed. Goddammit. Might as well spit it out. "I went to see Natasha."

Sarah's eyes grew wide. "Wow. You must really love her."

Mac let out a huff, and Billy blinked at the noise. Sarah didn't mean Natasha, and they both knew it. "I think the lack of sleep is catching up with you."

"I have mother's intuition now. Good luck getting anything past me." She squinted. "So are you going to tell me what Natasha said, or do I have to wheedle that out of you too?"

Mac paced the room as he held Billy. How was he supposed to talk to Sarah about it when he didn't even know what to think? "Natasha told me it's okay to have what I want."

"Does that mean you know what you want?" Sarah gave him a knowing smile. "Or should I say, who you want?"

Mac let out a sigh. Of course he knew. Everyone seemed to know. Except for the one woman who should because he hadn't had the gumption to tell her. "It's not that easy. I screwed up."

Sarah stood and took Billy from him. "It is that easy. You literally have a plane. Go to her."

Mac groaned. This was why he avoided family time. He could never get away with anything. "Why are you busting my chops?"

Sarah settled back down onto the couch, cradling Billy. "Because you called me out on my BS, and I'm returning the favor." She looked him in the eye. "Do you want to be with Elle or not?"

He swallowed, his throat thick. Wanting her wasn't the problem. "What if she doesn't want to be with me?"

"There's only one way to find out."

Mac rubbed the back of his neck. Exhaustion seeped through his bones. But was he tired from daily life or from resisting the pull of what he wanted?

His gaze drifted out the window. Mac took in the thick

trees, remembering that day in the forest when Elle had cried her eyes out. He could still feel her pressed against him, wishing he could absorb every ounce of pain and make it all better.

Mac had told her then that Travis had free will. That he made his own choices. Just like Mac's parents made their choice to be in Alaska. Or Sarah made her choice to come back to Darling. Or how Grace decided to get divorced and move here too. Everyone had decided for themselves. So why was Mac trying to decide for Elle?

Mac looked back at Sarah. "Can you watch the dog for a few days?"

Her face lit up, a little smug for his liking. Wasn't it enough that women were always right? Did they have to rub it in too? "I hope you mean what I think you mean."

Mac gave a firm nod. He had promised Elle he'd get her old life back. But he had to break that promise to make her a much bigger one: to love her forever. "I reckon I'll leave as soon as I make a few phone calls. Gotta get my flights covered."

Sarah squealed, and the baby babbled along with her. "I think this is the bravest thing you've ever done."

"Go to California again?"

She let out a laugh. "Tell someone you need them."

Mac swallowed. As long as he was asking questions, he might as well ask for help too. "Can you get her address for me?"

Sarah sighed. "I guess I can break a rule this one time. But you better not go falling in love with every guest who walks through the door."

Mac shook his head. "She's the only one for me."

Sarah smiled at him. "I think you've perfected your apology speech."

He kissed the baby and gave his sister a hug. Mac rubbed

the husky on the head and promised to be back, hopefully with another human.

A flicker of hope spurted to life in his heart. Natasha had said they only get to do this once. But with the right person by his side, once would be enough.

CHAPTER TWENTY-NINE

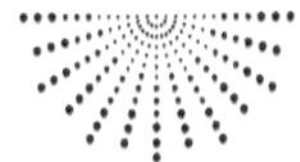

ELLE

Elle's face hurt. She had been smiling for hours, which, under the best of circumstances, was exhausting. Doing it while her heart was breaking made it that much harder.

It had been a month since she had seen Mac. Almost four times as long as the time they'd spent together. Shouldn't it be getting easier by now? Not harder?

The photographer lowered his camera. "Okay, let's try it with you holding the cookbook again."

The makeup artist walked out onto the set. "I just need a minute." She dabbed more concealer under Elle's eyes. "Your shirt holding up okay?"

Elle reached back and felt the pin where the wardrobe assistant had gathered her top. "All good."

She picked up the cookbook, and the camera kept snapping.

Her body ached. She was tired, back to her old tricks of working too much and resting too little. Not to mention, her appetite had disappeared, which didn't exactly inspire her to create new recipes.

But her followers had missed her and were hungry for more. Lacey had hugged Elle as she told her that they had signed another cookbook deal and the miniseries was still on the table.

Elle had thought she'd come back to a ghost of her former career. But her brand was more popular than ever. Even though her presence on social media had been minimal during her time in Darling, Lacey hadn't been joking when she had said people liked the Alaskan content. Not even the news of her breakup with Travis had seemed to affect her numbers nor the enthusiasm for the miniseries. Thanks to her trending status, the producer had been happy to scrap the couple's angle and focus solely on her.

So Elle smiled at the camera. Maybe she wasn't happy. But she couldn't let this career slip away from her. She had already lost so much.

Just when Elle was ready to collapse, the photographer put the camera down again. "Okay, I think I have enough. Let's call it a day."

Elle thanked him and gathered her things to head home. She couldn't wait to scrub away the layers of makeup. It all seemed so ridiculous. At the beginning of the day, she created a personality. At the end of the day, she washed it off. In between, no one ever saw the real Elle Blessing.

As she walked down the hallway to her condo, an unfamiliar number popped up on her phone.

Her heart sped up. The number was registered to Alaska.

Elle's finger shook as she swiped the screen. "Hello?"

"Elle? It's Sarah."

Her shoulders sagged. Did she really think Mac would call? He hadn't even told her goodbye when she walked off his plane. "Sarah." Elle forced a smile, trying to keep the disappointment out of her voice. "It's so nice to hear from you."

"We miss you around here. I'm still so bummed I didn't get to tell you goodbye." Sarah cleared her throat, apparently realizing that wasn't a welcome topic. "Anyway, I'm calling about Dickinson. No one has claimed her. Would you like her? I can send her to you. I already checked with the airline."

The knife in Elle's heart twisted. One of the last tenuous connections to the love of her life, and he didn't even want it. "That's really nice of you to ask, but it's too hot in LA for a husky."

In the background, a baby wailed. Elle's chest tightened, remembering the day Billy had been born. And the night she had spent with Mac after. The night Elle had thought changed everything. But she had been wrong.

Sarah let out a sigh. "I have to go. I'll call again later."

Elle took a shaky breath as she slipped the phone back into her purse. Maybe she wouldn't answer next time. The less she held on, the better.

She pulled out her keys and unlocked the door to her condo. Elle waited to feel the tension drain from her shoulders, for her breath to get a little deeper. But the sanctuary she used to find here was gone.

Elle swallowed. She was going to have to move. If her new apartment looked like a shop in Alaska, so be it. Maybe she should get a dog too. She did miss the husky, even if she had told Sarah the truth. It was too hot in LA for Dickinson. But more than that, Elle wasn't strong enough to have the memory of Mac around her every day.

She opened the fridge and reached for the bottle of Barbera. Elle took her glass to the window, looking out over the city. She used to love this view. But now she preferred rocky beaches and thick forest trees.

Her eyes burned. For a moment, she had let herself dream

that her life could be different. But the thing about dreams was that eventually you wake up.

Elle wiped at her eyes, remembering the look on Mac's face the last time she saw him. She had glanced back as she stepped off the plane, giving him one last chance he hadn't taken.

She took a sip of wine, hoping that would get rid of the lump in her throat. Why had he done it? Why had Mac pushed her away?

Elle tightened her grip on the wineglass. It didn't matter if she didn't want this life anymore. She didn't have anything, anyone else besides this career. And Elle wouldn't give it up for someone who wasn't willing to fight for her.

She shook her head. Change both their lives for a summer fling? If she wasn't so heartbroken, it would be laughable.

Her phone pinged. Elle walked over and grabbed it from her purse. It was a message from Lacey asking about setting up another meeting for next week.

Elle's stomach churned, and the wine turned sour in her mouth. She tossed the phone back into her purse and went to the kitchen.

She poured the rest of the wine out in the sink and set the glass aside. Resting her hands against the counter, Elle hung her head. She hated herself. She hated herself for still hurting.

With a deep breath, Elle went back over to her purse. She texted Lacey that she'd take the meeting. It was the last window of free time Elle had left in her week, but she didn't care. The more work, the better. The more work, the less time to think.

She brushed her teeth and did her skin care, piling on the moisturizer and serums. With the miniseries back on the table, the topic of getting her face done had come up again. Elle had nothing against it, but she didn't think she needed it.

Elle gazed into the mirror, hearing Mac tell her that he liked her with nothing extra. Just herself.

Her shoulders drooped as she walked into the bedroom. Apparently, high-definition cameras said otherwise. Stress and lack of sleep definitely didn't help either.

Turning off the light, Elle listened to the thick silence of the dark. There was no soft snoring of a grown man or the whistling breath of a husky that never seemed to stop shedding.

Salty tears dripped onto her silk pillowcase. Squeezing her eyes shut, Elle pretended she was back on an island that no one knew about with the one person who saw her for who she wanted to be.

* * *

ELLE THANKED the driver and stepped out of the car. She wove her way through the crowd, heading to the restaurant for her next meeting. They all seemed to blend together, one after another.

She shaded her eyes against the sun. Elle missed the rain. Every day in LA had gorgeous weather. And somehow, it didn't seem as special.

The hostess showed her to a patio table, and Elle did a double take. "Travis?"

He stood, wrapping her in a hug. "It's good to see you."

"I'm having déjà vu." Elle pulled back, blinking at him. They hadn't spoken since he had moved out of the condo and she had given the ring back. "This is…you're not trying to get back together, are you?"

"No, definitely not." Travis shook his head, his cheeks

turning pink. "It was dumb to think we could go back to the way things were."

Elle gave him a sympathetic smile. "Then I'm dumb too. I had the same plan at first." She took a seat. "What is going on? Why did you want to meet?"

Travis sat back down. "I actually have a business proposition for you."

Elle lifted an eyebrow. This was a new side of him. "I'm listening."

Travis tilted his head, squinting into the sun. "Remember that fundraiser we met at? The one for the children's hospital?"

Elle nodded. She had thought all her dreams had come true the night Travis walked into her life. It was the safe, stable love she had always wanted. Now she realized that wasn't any kind of love at all. "Of course. I donated a cooking lesson, and you won." She let out a laugh. "You bid more than the winning bid for the trip to Paris."

"I had to get your attention somehow." He grinned as the server came over, bringing them glasses of ice water and taking their order. Travis got a chicken sandwich, and Elle ordered a salad. She should try to eat something today. Travis sipped his water. "I am actually volunteering with that hospital now, and we're working on this year's fundraiser."

"Oh my God, that's fantastic. I bet you're great at it."

He chuckled. "After all those years of my dad being on my case to grow up, it turns out I'm a natural at working with kids. Would you believe it?"

"I can imagine." She was genuinely happy for him.

Travis rubbed the back of his neck. "And it's nice to do something besides be someone's boyfriend for a change."

Elle shook her head, her stomach heavy with guilt. It had seemed so important then. But looking back, it had been ridiculous to waste all that time pretending. "I'm sorry. That wasn't fair to ask of you."

Travis held her gaze, his eyes rounded in apparent sympathy. "Then I guess I should apologize too. You deserved so much more than someone who just looked good in photos."

She leaned back in her chair, resting her hand against her forehead. "I wish we had talked about this before. We could've saved so much time."

The server came by with their food. Travis spread his napkin across his lap. "Better late than never, right?"

Elle swallowed. If only it wasn't too late for some things. "So back to the business proposition. How can I help?"

Travis picked up his sandwich. "Actually, I was wondering if you wanted to donate something again. It could really help us meet our goal. I feel like I've heard more about you than ever since you posted the Alaska stuff."

Elle's heart squeezed. She didn't want to talk about Alaska. Didn't want to think about it. "Maybe people were just excited to see something different."

Travis looked her in the eye. "I think it was the fact that you were happy."

Elle reached for her water, taking a gulp. She had thought she had been happy. But happiness didn't last.

Sometimes she saw a man with a beard who stood taller than the crowd. Her heart would hop into her throat, and for fifteen seconds, Elle believed in a happy ending. But this was real life. There were no happy endings, just happy moments.

Her phone pinged, and she squinted at the screen. Lacey again. Next week was officially booked solid too.

Elle slumped in her chair. Her back ached. Her heart ached. Her soul ached. She was officially full-time miserable.

Travis cleared his throat. "Hey. You okay?"

Elle slipped her phone back into her purse. "Yeah, just something for work."

"If you get sick of it, I can recommend running off into the forest to reevaluate." He took a bite of his sandwich. "Make sure to bring some food, though."

Elle let out a laugh, picking up her fork and spearing a cherry tomato. "Tempting. But I'm not sure that's exactly what I want right now."

Travis chuckled. "If you ever figure it out, let me know. I'll give you all my tips."

Elle smiled, looking down at her salad. She heard Mac asking her what she wanted. Her telling him that she didn't know and wishing that she did.

She sat up. That was true. She might not know what she wanted. But she knew what she *didn't* want.

This life.

This career.

And any man who wasn't Mac.

Elle set her fork down, her heart pounding. It was impossible to be happy all of the time. But even if happiness only lasted a moment, those moments made up a life worth living. "Travis? What if I donated everything?"

CHAPTER THIRTY

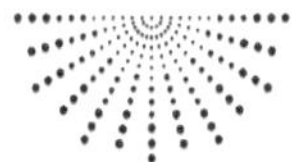

ELLE

Elle let out a huff as she set down the box, stacking it against the wall with the others. Her condo now looked more like a storage unit than a home. And almost all of it was going to the fundraiser.

The children's hospital had jumped at the chance to auction Elle's signature equipment and props. The plan was to recreate sets Elle had used in her content to display everything for the auction. Travis had told her that ticket sales had already hit a new record.

Elle grabbed the tape dispenser, stretching a sticky piece across the top of the box. Unlike the children's hospital, Lacey hadn't been as wild about the fundraiser idea. But that was fine because Elle didn't need a manager anymore. Not when she had no idea what she was doing. All she knew was that she didn't want to live a life that she had to talk herself into.

She set the tape dispenser aside and stuck a label on the box. In addition to Lacey, Elle had lost some followers when she announced the change in the direction of her platform. Apparently, not everyone was excited about getting to know a more authentic side of Elle. Luckily, she had a healthy savings account, and downsizing into a smaller apartment would also help.

Though the move to a smaller place was about more than cutting expenses. Elle didn't want to leave room for anyone in her life again. Everyone would be measured against Mac, and everyone would be found lacking.

The doorbell rang, and Elle pursed her lips. She had specifically blocked off this week to organize everything for the fundraiser and pack up the little she was keeping. As far as she knew, no one should be stopping by.

Elle checked the doorbell camera, and her pulse quickened. She opened the door slowly, as if the man who stood on the other side was a mirage and would disappear in a wisp of smoke. "Mac."

"Elle."

His voice tugged on her heartstrings, as sad and lonely as she felt. "What are you doing here?"

"Figured it was my turn to show up at your door unannounced." Mac cleared his throat. "Mind if I come in for a minute?"

She opened the door wider. Hopefully, he couldn't hear her heart pounding. "Of course."

He stepped inside, glancing at the boxes. "You're moving."

"More like downsizing. It's just me." Elle clasped her hands together, her face warm. It wasn't like that was news to Mac. He had been the one to let her walk away. "Can I get you something to drink? A glass of wine? If you don't mind a plastic cup."

Mac lifted a shoulder. "I can't drink. I might be flying later."

Elle frowned. Mac had made it clear how he felt about

LA. She was surprised he had stepped foot in town without an exit plan. "Might?"

"It depends," he said, his voice thick. "On what you say."

She swallowed, telling herself not to get her hopes up. "About what?"

He reached for her hand and pulled her to him. She landed against his hard chest with a thump, his touch sending a jolt of electricity through her. "Just in case it's the last time," he whispered.

Mac cradled her face, lowering his mouth to hers and kissing her like his life depended on it.

Her head spun, and Elle pulled back with a gasp. She reached up to touch her lips, certain they were on fire. What was going on? What was Mac doing here, kissing her until her toes curled? "I'm so confused right now. How do you even know where I live?"

His cheeks turned pink. "I got your address from your reservation. I know that's not right. Report me if you want. I'd rather sit in jail than have to live wondering about you. About us."

Her heart slammed into her ribs. *Us.* "What about us?"

Mac ran his hand through his hair. "The thing is, Elle, now that you're gone, I find I can't very well live without you. It's stupid, I know. I barely know you. But I am a stupid man, or I would've never let you go. I miss you. The town misses you. The damn dog misses you."

He shook his head. "Darling isn't LA. I don't really know what kind of cooking star you could be up there. We could get a better house, of course, with a nice kitchen. Though I know a kitchen can't replace all this. But I wanted to ask in case it's enough." His voice cracked, and her heart jerked. "In case I'm enough. "

She held in her breath as he reached into his back pocket and pulled out a ring box. Mac opened it, revealing a simple gold band. "What I am trying to say is that I love you. I want to be with you. So I'm going to ask you the question I should've asked before you left. Will you, Elle Blessing, take me, Maverick Carter, to be your husband?"

Elle looked into Mac's eyes, and she saw it. She saw her whole life, and she knew there was only one answer she could give. "Yes. I love you too, Maverick Carter. Take me home."

He let out a whoop and wrapped his arms around her, spinning her in a circle. When he set her down, Mac pulled the ring from the box and placed it on her finger with a shaking hand. "It's engraved. Damn miracle too. You really can get anything in Los Angeles."

She stared at the ring on her finger, not able to bring herself to take it off right away. "What does it say?"

"It's my promise to you. One I intend to keep for the rest of my life." Mac pressed a kiss to her temple, and Elle closed her eyes, her heart memorizing the moment. "Are you sure you don't want me to move to Los Angeles? I could probably do it with a regular delivery of Wolfie's beer. It's not fair for you to start all over."

Elle blinked her eyes open, looking up at him. Starting all over. It was something that she knew about. Except this time, she wasn't starting over for safety or security or success. She was starting over to be happy. "Nah. I'm already packed."

Mac chuckled, the deep, throaty sound sending a tingle to her toes. "In that case, I will have some of that wine. Because I'm going to stick around and help. There's no way I am leaving without you. Sarah won't mind watching Dickinson for a few more days."

He walked to the kitchen. Elle slipped the ring off, holding it up to the light and squinting at the inside band.

True love is forever.

Her heart swelled. Some things don't change. Some things are forever.

Elle turned and looked out the window, taking in the view of Los Angeles one more time. She had achieved almost everything she had ever wanted here, only to discover it wasn't what she really wanted at all.

"I have a question for you," Mac said behind her.

Elle turned, taking a glass of wine from him. "What's that?"

Mac took a gulp of his drink. "Now that we're getting married, will you finally tell me where you're from? It's been driving me nuts."

Elle lifted the corner of her mouth. "I guess I can put you out of your misery. I grew up in Minnesota."

He grinned, and she mirrored his expression. It was impossible not to be happy when he was happy. "I guess that means you can pitch in with the snow shoveling. I can't imagine a more perfect woman for life in Alaska." Mac sighed. "I don't know how I got so lucky."

Elle fluttered her eyelashes at him. "To meet me?"

He flashed a teasing smile. "To meet anyone."

"Ouch." She giggled, giving him a nudge. "Can we really get a new house?"

"I'm shocked." Mac splayed his hand against his chest. "I thought my house was the reason you were willing to move to Darling."

Elle placed a hand on her hip, shaking her head. "It's not right for a family."

Mac's face lit up. "You're right. We need room for ten kids at least."

Her jaw dropped. Ten little Mavericks? She'd be the one needing a regular delivery of Wolfie's beer. "No way. I don't want to be outnumbered. Two kids total."

"Deal." Mac gave a firm nod. "You know, this city is

growing on me. Last time, I got my sister back. Now, I've got you. Not quite the shanty town of broken dreams I thought it was."

Elle took a sip of her wine. "That's ironic. My dreams are coming true by leaving."

Mac rubbed the back of his neck. "What about your work? I don't ever want to stand in the way of your success."

"Already taken care of." Elle slipped her phone from her pocket, pulling up her latest post announcing her shift to a more authentic platform. She handed it to Mac. "Read this."

His gaze flicked back and forth, and she swore his eyes glistened. "You really are fearless, you know that?"

Elle took the phone back, sticking it in her pocket. She wasn't sure if she was fearless or foolish. But either way, it was better than being too afraid to make any choice at all. "You said it yourself: that job did not make me happy. The most fun I had cooking in years was in Darling. I don't know what I'll do now. But I'll figure it out. Either people will follow me, or they won't."

Mac nuzzled her neck, his breath tickling her ear and sending a shiver through her. "As long as that's what you want."

Elle rested her head against his firm chest, letting out a sigh. This was home. "I've never been more sure of anything in my life."

He wrapped his free arm around her and held her close. "Same here, sweetheart."

Her heart squeezed, heavy and full. After years of creating a life that was appealing to millions of strangers, she was doing the bravest thing she had ever done. She was creating the life that she wanted.

CHAPTER THIRTY-ONE

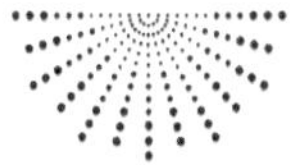

ELLE

Will spread the blueprint out on the kitchen island. "I finished all the revisions from our last meeting. What do you think?"

Elle looked over the plan, her body buzzing with energy. They had started designing their new home when she first got back to Darling. After two months, they had finally finished. "It's perfect."

Mac reached for her hand, giving it a squeeze. "A perfect home for a perfect woman."

Sarah and Will exchanged a look before Sarah turned back to Mac. "No more giving us crap about being too lovey-dovey ever again. You're making my morning sickness come back."

Mac scowled. "What? This is what you wanted. Let me be happy."

Will cleared his throat as he rolled up the plans. He never got between the Carter siblings, and Elle had decided he was a wise man. "I'm not exactly sure how long construction will take. You know how the weather is here. But at least you have it to look forward to, whenever it's done."

Elle nodded. It seemed like she had nothing but things to look forward to these days. When she had first come to Darling, Elle thought her life had fallen apart. Looking back, it was actually the beginning of something so much better. "I can't wait."

Sarah picked up her teacup. "Well, let's talk about something that is happening soon. Can you believe it's only a month until the wedding?" She glanced at Billy sleeping in his playpen. "I hope you don't mind that your ring bearer is going to be accompanied by your construction manager. But it's the only way Billy can get down the aisle."

Elle shook her head. They had discussed having the wedding next year. By then, Billy might be able to walk himself. But now that she finally knew what she wanted, Elle didn't want to wait that long. "I think Will is the perfect addition to the wedding party. It'll help keep things even. After all, our flower girl has four legs."

Sarah smiled, sipping her tea. "I ordered Dickinson's bow last week. It should be getting here soon."

Mac let out a groan. "We are going to need that open bar nice and early."

Elle nudged him gently with her elbow. "Not too early. You better remember this."

"Sweetheart, I remember everything about you." Mac held her gaze, and her pulse quickened.

Before Elle could say anything, Sarah stood from the kitchen island. "Maybe I should leave you two alone to plan the honeymoon."

Mac stuck his tongue out. "Already done. I couldn't talk Elle into getting on a plane, so we're taking the ferry over to Sitka for a couple of nights."

Elle held up her hands. "The plane back to Darling was the last one for me."

Sarah gathered the dirty cups. "You should talk to Natasha about Sitka. That's where she's from, you know."

A shiver traveled down Elle's spine, and she looked at Mac.

You have met the man you will marry.

"She was right." He quirked up the corner of his mouth.

Elle's heart stretched in her chest. She loved that he knew her so well, even if that meant he also knew the most effective ways to annoy her. "I guess we better get going. I'm trying out a new recipe tonight, and Mac promised to help."

He narrowed his eyes. "And I was promised a stop at the Buck first."

Elle clapped her hands, and Dickinson came running. "Exactly. We can't stop there if we don't get going."

After telling Will and Sarah goodbye, they headed out to the truck. The husky sat in the middle, of course. Elle had made the mistake of having Dickinson jump in the truck bed once, and Mac had looked horrified. It had taken everything Elle had not to laugh. Mac really was all bark and no bite, and the *damn dog* was officially part of the family.

He started the engine and pulled away from the lodge. "Still got a good bit of light left. Mind taking a spin by the place?"

She smiled, resting her head against the seat back. "I'd love to."

They drove up the road, the fiery sunset reaching through the trees and cutting a pattern on the inside of the cab. Halfway between the lodge and town, Mac slowed the truck and pulled over. "Home sweet home."

Elle's stomach fluttered. There wasn't much to see right now. Just a patch of land that split the difference between being close to family and Mac's shop. But Elle didn't need a house to know she was home. All she needed was one grumpy pilot and a husky that never stopped shedding.

As she stepped out of the truck, her phone rang and interrupted the thick silence of the forest. It was her new manager, Charlie. Elle looked up at Mac. "Sorry."

He shooed her away. "Take as much time as you need. You know I'm not going anywhere."

Elle blew him a kiss before answering. "Hey, Charlie. What's going on?"

Charlie squealed, and Elle held the phone away from her ear. "They accepted the proposal!"

Elle stopped in her tracks, her body numb. Her Alaskan content had been doing so well that she and Charlie had taken a different proposal back to the producer of the miniseries, one focused on the kind of work she did now. But they weren't supposed to hear back from the producer for another week. Elle shoved the phone against her ear. Had she heard that right? "They did?"

"Mm-hmm." Charlie hummed. "I'm emailing you everything right now to sign, but wait until you hear their offer."

Charlie rattled off the number, and Elle's eyes practically rolled back in her head. With that kind of money, they could get the house finished as quickly as construction could be done. She bit her lip. It had to be too good to be true. "What's the catch? Do I have to travel to LA or something?"

She dreaded even the thought of flying. Elle knew Mac wouldn't like her being gone all the time either.

"No catch," Charlie said. "They just want you to be yourself."

Elle swallowed. All this time, she had been doing it wrong. She never had to be anyone else. And once she had finally gotten the courage to admit what she wanted, it seemed all her dreams came true. "Thank you for the good news, Charlie. Let's go over all the details on Monday."

They ended the call, and Elle slipped the phone back into her pocket. Work could wait. She had a life to live.

Elle made her way across the property, measuring out the rooms with each step.

This was the hallway. She could hear little feet pitter-pattering against the hardwood floors.

This was the kitchen. She could taste the homemade pancakes.

This was the living room. She could see the Christmas tree in the corner.

Mac waited for her there. Elle sucked in a breath at the sight of him. It wasn't the promise of what was to come that made her heart soar. It was the promise of creating it with the love of her life.

He tilted his head. "Everything good?"

Elle slipped her arm through his. Dickinson trotted over, apparently not wanting to be left out. She plopped to a sit next to Elle. "Just perfect. I'll tell you all about it later."

Mac held Elle close as they gazed out at the dark water. It wrapped around countless wild islands and kissed the rocky beaches. "Speaking of perfect, what a view, huh?"

She pressed into him. From here, it felt like they were standing on the edge of time, the beginning, middle, and end stretching out in all directions. And she wanted to share every minute with Mac.

"It is pretty nice." Elle pulled away and turned her back to the water. She reached up, gently resting a hand against the side of Mac's face. "But this is the view of Alaska that I fell in love with."

EPILOGUE

ELLE

Elle pulled back the curtain and peeked out the window. Her stomach fluttered. Based on the size of the crowd that had gathered outside, it seemed like all of Darling had shown up for their wedding.

She smiled to herself. Not only did everyone show up, but they had pitched in too. A group had come over yesterday to decorate the lodge. Every guest had brought a potluck dish to contribute to the wedding feast. And Wolfie had agreed to both officiate and serve drinks after the ceremony. The only person who had declined to join was Natasha, though they had invited her.

With a sigh, Elle dropped the curtain and walked back over to the mirror. Every day, she woke up to find herself happier than the day before. A year ago, she wouldn't have thought it was possible. Now, she couldn't imagine living any other way.

She rested her hand over her heart, closing her eyes. How strange life was. How wonderful.

A knock came at the door, and she snapped her eyes open. Sarah poked her head in. "You aren't getting cold feet, are you?"

Elle shook her head. "Just the opposite."

"Thank goodness. I'd hate to lose both a sister-in-law and our new chef in one day." Sarah clasped her hands together. "It'll be so fun to work together next summer. Especially for the guests. I assume they prefer when the food is edible."

Elle let out a laugh, something she seemed to do more often these days. Cooking at the lodge gave her both a creative outlet and a fantastic setting for her new platform, including filming for the miniseries. It was also a huge help to Sarah, who claimed she wasn't much of a cook even without a newborn keeping her up all night. "I'm having fun already. I don't remember the last time I was this inspired."

"Love will do that to you." Sarah winked as she adjusted one of the fireweed blossoms that dotted Elle's updo. Compared to the simple white dress and flats, Elle's hair was the most complicated part of her outfit. The bright pink blossoms matched her bouquet. "There. Now it's perfect."

Elle watched her in the mirror. "Speaking of perfect, it's really not fair that you got your figure back so quickly."

Sarah waved her hand. "It's going to be the same for you when you have children. Mac, however, will be ruined. He'll be a full-time softie."

Elle giggled. She had no doubt. She could tell from the way Mac played with his nephew that he adored kids.

Her heart squeezed. Their nephew. Some people still didn't understand why Elle had left everything behind in LA. But she had gained so much more when she moved to Darling, including a family. She had a brother and a sister and even parents again, now that Diana and Richard Carter were back from Italy. She had loved Sarah and Mac's parents the minute she had met them.

Sarah reached out her hand, her eyes glistening. "Ready?"

She took Sarah's hand and gave it a squeeze. Elle couldn't wait to start the rest of her life with Mac. "More than ready."

They made their way down the stairs and out to the front porch, stepping into the bright summer afternoon. The sun shone down, warm and hopeful. A breeze whistled through the trees, the scent of spruce mixing with the salty sea air. The day couldn't be more perfect if it had been put together by a set designer. But the only part Elle cared about was the man waiting for her at the end of the aisle.

Sarah caught Charlotte's eye, giving her a nod. The music started, and the crowd hushed as they turned to face Elle.

Will and Billy made their way down the aisle first. Dickinson trotted behind them, her fireweed pink bow bouncing with each step. After one last hug from Sarah, it was Elle's turn.

With a deep breath, she carefully, slowly, placed one foot in front of the other. Elle counted in her head, pacing herself. It took everything she had not to run and jump into Mac's arms.

When she finally reached the end of the aisle, Mac leaned forward and kissed her right on the mouth. Elle melted into him, looping her arms around his neck. The bouquet hit the ground with a thud.

The crowd let out a gasp, and Wolfie cleared his throat loudly. "It's not time yet," he grumbled.

Mac pulled away, scowling at him. "I've been waiting my whole life for this moment. Five more minutes were out of the question."

Everyone laughed, and Wolfie threw his hands in the air. "I'll do the short version, then."

"Why didn't you say that was an option in the first place?" Mac leaned down to pick up Elle's bouquet. He handed it to her with a wink. "Guess we still need this for a couple more minutes. Apparently, there are rules about these things."

After they exchanged vows and rings, Wolfie gave Mac a pointed look. "You may *now* kiss the bride."

Mac pulled Elle close, wrapping his arm around her waist. "Finally," he whispered before kissing her silly again.

The crowd let out another cheer, punctuated with a few hoots and whistles for good measure.

They broke apart, and Elle giggled, practically bursting with happiness. Here she was, a million miles away from everything she knew, and yet she had never felt more at home.

Mac took the bouquet from Elle and passed it to Charlotte. Elle glanced over her shoulder as the bunch of fireweed disappeared behind her. "What are you doing?"

"I've never been one for tradition, but I think the first dance is ours." Mac took Elle's hand and led her out onto the dance floor. "Besides, if I don't take my turn now, I may never get it. There's a line of men with broken hearts waiting for their consolation dance with you. "

Elle faced him, placing her other hand on his broad shoulder. "What about the women with broken hearts?"

He snorted. "No such thing."

Elle shook her head. "You realize we have a lifetime together. We'll have plenty of time to do it all."

Mac tightened his grip on her waist, and her pulse quickened. "Be that as it may, I don't intend to waste a moment."

He spun her around the dance floor, and Elle let out a gasp. She had no idea Mac knew how to dance. "You never fail to surprise me. Do you know that?"

Mac threw his head back and laughed. "Lady, you could say the feeling is mutual. I remember seeing you step off that plane, and I thought you were an angel. Then you talked to me, and I decided you came from underground."

He dipped her low. "But then things changed again, and somehow, I fell in love."

Elle straightened. "That definitely wasn't part of the plan."

Mac crinkled his eyes, and her breath hitched. She'd never get used to that smile. "Let go of the plan. Real life is so much better."

She tilted her head. He wasn't getting off easy just because it was their wedding day. "That's rich coming from the man who planned on everything always staying the same."

Mac held her gaze, his voice husky. "You taught me that was a life too boring to live. You taught me everything."

Her chest tightened. Then it was a fair trade. Because before Mac, she hadn't really lived at all.

Before she could answer, a few stray raindrops dotted the dance floor. Elle looked up, squinting in the glare of the gray sky. Clouds had rolled in and cloaked the sun.

Sarah cupped her hands together, raising her voice. "Alright, folks. Looks like we're taking this party inside."

As the rain fell faster, everyone rushed to gather what they could carry and duck inside the lodge. Bart and Dickinson followed the crowd, tails wagging. In an impressive feat of teamwork, Will and Wolfie made sure that the kegs weren't left behind.

Mac grabbed Elle's hand, and they raced to take cover under the porch. He chuckled as the rain drummed against the awning. "I guess it wouldn't be an authentic Alaskan wedding without a little rain."

Elle rested her head against his shoulder as they stood there, gazing out into the downpour. "That's okay. The sunshine will be back eventually."

* * *

A NOTE FROM THE AUTHOR

Thank you for taking the time to read my book. I hope you had as much fun reading it as I did writing it.

If you did enjoy it, and want to help other people discover Elle and Mac's story, please consider leaving a review at the retailer where you purchased this book. It would absolutely make my day (especially if share who your favorite character is!).

Thank you kindly.

ACKNOWLEDGMENTS

This section could easily be longer than the rest of the book twice over, but I feel like that might be disappointing to those of you who thought there was more to Mac and Elle's story. So instead, I'll do my best to keep it short and sweet.

To Sarah, for having the patience of a saint and the wisdom of, well, a saint. Thank you for helping me get this story where it needed to be. We didn't take the most direct route, but hey, we got there.

To Sandra, for having an eagle eye. Thank you for putting the final polish on this book. You rock!

To the team at Best Page Forward, for once again creating a visual masterpiece and for putting the most perfect short and sweet words to the story. I seriously don't know how you do it, but I am so thankful you do.

To Jen, for talking me out of giving up. You made everything seem less impossible when I was thisclose to running into the forest myself and never looking back. I appreciate your time and compassionate words.

To my mom, who spent hours with me on the phone while I worked through this book. I could not have done it without you. Perhaps there were some days when not finishing the story would've been more merciful to both of us.

To Danelle, for setting the standard a little too high. I shouldn't compare others to you, but it's impossible. There is no comparison.

Thank you all.

ABOUT THE AUTHOR

Lark Holiday is the author of feel-good and funny romances. She lives in California with her opinionated dogs and her human family. When she's not writing, she spends her time going for walks, vacuuming dog hair, and feeling like she should probably be writing.

Though Lark is based in California now, she lived in Alaska many times over the past few decades. Her time in The Last Frontier inspired the Darling Men series.